T0105699

IN THE SHADOW OF THE LION

KIMBERLY M. JANE

abbott press®

A DIVISION OF WRITER'S DIGEST

IN THE SHADOW OF THE LION

Abbott Press books may be ordered through booksellers or by contacting:

Abbott Press
1663 Liberty Drive
Bloomington, IN 47403
www.abbottpress.com
Phone: 1-866-697-5310

ISBN: 978-1-4582-0620-6 (sc)
ISBN: 978-1-4582-0622-0 (hc)
ISBN: 978-1-4582-0621-3 (e)

Library of Congress Control Number: 2012918400

Printed in the United States of America

Abbott Press rev. date: 11/5/2012

In loving memory of James Shearsby

I will never forget how your wonderful smile and
great sense of humour brightened my day. Your light will shine
forever in my heart.

I saw what happened to her, but not only that, I felt her pain, her hatred, her anguish, and her lust for revenge.

—Kathleen Gallant

CONTENTS

ACKNOWLEDGMENTS

I would like to acknowledge my husband and best friend, Kirk J. Shearsby, for his support and patience, his limitless assistance, and his brilliant literary mind.

Thanks to Kaleigh, Jalen, and Alexander for their inspiration.

Thank you to my parents for their love and support, encouraging me to never give up.

Thank you to Loraine Shearsby and her husband, the late James Shearsby. Their strength and dedication gave me the courage to endure the mountainous task of completing the first of many novels.

I would like to thank my friends Juli Towne-Gurski and Heather Leenders and my childhood friend Johanne Grenier for their support and encouragement. They have always believed in me.

Special thanks to Mike Wells for all his support and assistance.

Special thanks to my friend Kevin Almeida for offering his photographic talent.

CHAPTER 1

THE GUARDIANS

"Jaja! Jaja!" cried the mother as she ran out of her home, her long wraparound dress fluttering in the evening breeze. Darkness crept over the golden savannah, transforming it into a myriad of shadows. The crickets' night chorus reassured her that she was safe.

She stood at the edge of the grass, searching the landscape for any sign of her son.

She called out his name. Silence fell upon her ears. The soft breeze rustled the turf. An overwhelming wave of hysteria threatened to overcome her, but she held strong. He had played this game before, but this night she sensed a presence.

The foul scent of a predator nearby sent a surge of panic racing through her. She ran into the waist-high, straw-like grass, her eyes desperately searching the shadows as she raced against nightfall.

The sun touched the horizon.

Alone and surrounded by a sea of towering grass, the naked toddler clumsily stumbled forward, squealing in delight each time he heard his mother call his name. He lost his balance and fell face-first onto a patch of dry dirt. He then pushed himself back up onto his tiny feet.

A fell cackle startled him. The toddler stood still and listened. The grass rustled, parting before him. The silhouette of a hyena emerged from the shadows. Teeth bared, it seemed to smile at him.

The boy whimpered.

The animal moved closer.

The boy began to wail.

The boy's mother stopped and listened; she heard him. She ran in the direction of his voice.

Others from the tribe joined the search. Torches and spears in their hands, their voices carried into the night. Suddenly, a deafening roar froze them.

The mother screamed. She searched blindly through her tears, afraid that her worst fear had been realized. She stopped and leaned over to catch her breath. She was on the verge of collapsing when a woman reached out and caught her. With her support, the mother found the strength and courage to continue. They followed the men, who were marching in formation until they suddenly stopped. The mother broke away from the woman's hold, stumbled forward, and pushed herself between two men. At the sight of her son, she dropped to her knees and began to pray out loud.

A lion stood over the body of her child, the wind blowing its golden mane as it lifted its head against the crimson sky. It bellowed loudly before stepping over the toddler and disappearing into the tall grass.

The men shouted and immediately began charging after it, determined to kill the beast.

She ran over to her son and lifted him up into her arms, tears streaking her dirt-stained cheeks. Her baby opened his eyes and smiled. She squeezed his little body against hers and rocked him back and forth, crying. She quickly examined him for cuts and bruises but thankfully found only a small scratch on his shoulder.

Feeling safe in his mother's arms, the boy snuggled his face against her neck. He had lifted his head to look at the red sky when he saw the hyena again, standing atop a small termite hill. The child had the strange feeling that it was smiling at him. A small cry escaped his lips before he buried his face in her hair. His mother gently stroked her fingers through his curly hair, soothing him. While she carried him home, he fell asleep in her arms.

*   *   *

Even after spending several hours in a tanning salon, the locals still stared at her. At five foot six, she was one of the tallest in her class back home, but here, many teenagers surpassed her height, so she didn't believe it was that that drew their attention. The people mostly stared at her straight, thick mane of long, blonde hair, gleaming in the sunlight, which accentuated her golden complexion.

She glanced beyond her onlookers to study the surrounding landscape. In the distance, away from the bustling excitement of the village, she saw the savannah. Scorched grass and red soil painted the scene for miles ahead of her. Small groves of acacias grew sparsely across the terrain before reaching the base of tall, majestic mountains, which were partially hidden by haze.

A sudden tug on her shirt brought her attention back to the small village. A little boy had reached out to touch her strange-looking hair when his mother caught sight of him. In a desperate attempt to stop her son, she crossed the dirt road quickly, accidentally knocking over the fruit basket of a woman passing by. Frustrated, she stopped to help gather the fruit, apologizing to the woman while keeping a close eye on her son.

The blonde girl crouched to meet the child and smiled.

The child smiled in turn, stroking her hair.

The mother, who had finished gathering the runaway fruits, grabbed her son's hand and began speaking to him very quickly, seemingly reprimanding him.

"It's all right; no harm was done," she said to the mother, who was hastily rushing away with her son.

She stood up and saw a Caucasian girl and boy standing close to her with their oversized backpacks hanging from their shoulders.

A weathered school bus approached before screeching to a halt. The doors opened and the bus driver, an African man in his late forties, shouted words unfamiliar to her. He then cocked his head to one side, as if the unnecessary effort of speaking English annoyed him.

"Are you waitin' for the bus to take you to archaeological site, in Tsavo East National Park?" he huffed.

"Yes, I am," she answered. She immediately grabbed her backpack and sleeping bag before stepping onto the bus.

The moment she stepped inside, the occupants of the bus went silent. All of the seats at the back were taken, and when she went to sit beside a girl, the girl immediately stretched her legs out on the seat and stared defiantly back at her. Others copied her, allowing no place for the newcomer to sit.

"Okay, find a seat. We don't 'ave all day!" shouted the bus driver.

She turned around and saw the Caucasian girl and boy standing behind her, waiting to find seats for themselves.

The grumpy bus driver shouted something in his mother tongue.

The defiant girl who had denied her a seat grabbed a small bundle before leaving to sit beside someone else.

The blonde quickly slipped into the empty seat and stared out the window.

Another boy left his seat to join someone else, giving the other Caucasian teens a place to sit as well.

The driver ground the gears, and the bus jerked forward before accelerating. Soon the passengers began talking loudly amongst each other in their native tongue.

This was a stupid idea, she thought. *I could have spent my summer being a leader at the summer camp, with my best friend, Lucy, but instead I just had to look for adventure in a strange country. At least it's only for the month of August while Dad works in Nairobi on that stupid telecommunications project.*

The bus came to a stop fifteen minutes later.

She looked out the window to see a plump, dark boy cross in front of the bus.

"Ooh! He's goin' to need the whole seat!" shouted the defiant girl.

The other passengers laughed, except for the Caucasian girl and boy, who seemed intimidated and anxious.

"He must be a greedy American, this one!" shouted the defiant girl.

"What do they feed them in America?" shouted another.

The boy entered and stood before them, unsure of where to sit.

The blonde girl motioned for him to join her.

The teen gave her a large smile and sat beside her, tucking his backpack under his seat.

"Thank you."

"Don't mention it!" she answered.

"Not too friendly, are they?"

"No, especially that one." She turned around to look at the girl, whose dark hair was tightly braided in rows.

"What's up, buttercup?" quipped the defiant girl, when their eyes met.

The blonde girl turned around again before looking out the window.

"My name is Okechuku," he said, introducing himself.

"I'm Kathleen."

*   *   *

"Near the district of Mwitika, a lion has claimed a young man's life, making this the third death in one month . . ." blared the radio as the jeep traveled over the eroded, teeth-rattling dirt road.

Femi turned off the radio.

"I was listening to that," complained Sekani.

Femi looked at his son briefly before returning his eyes to the road.

"Don't believe everything you hear, Sekani," he said.

He watched his dad sway from side to side while the vehicle bounced over potholes.

Sekani stared out the window at the savannah. He understood why his father didn't want to listen to the news; he was infuriated by all the negative attention the lions were getting recently, and now some of the locals were taking it upon themselves to shoot them on sight.

Kanzikuta, a small town on the outskirts of Tsavo East National Park, was popular with many travelers. Tailored for tourists, this little pocket of stores sold everything from practical essentials to clothing, and for the more serious adventurers, hiking and camping equipment.

For the travelers who sought to buy souvenirs, gift shops were adorned with detailed local woodcarvings of animals and people, depicting stories of legendary gods and mythological creatures.

Tucked away behind a row of stores, almost hidden from view, was the Kanzikuta library. The wandering visitor would not take a second glance at the old run-down building, which seemed quite fine with the old librarian and his family. Some say that the library was a façade and that Mr. Galimi was hiding something behind the dusty shelves laden with old books and their tattered covers, magazines with torn pages, and newspapers with missing sections.

They pulled in front of the Kanzikuta General Store.

The general store was the main source of revenue for the small town. Stocked with a large selection of consumables, supplies, and equipment, it also served as an outpost for locals: being a communication center, a post office, and a drop zone for charitable donations from communities and businesses around the world, Kanzikuta General Store was a valuable resource for anyone who knew it existed. But for most, it was considered a store where you could purchase water, matches, T-shirts, or cold refreshing beverage.

Isolated with nothing around for miles, Kanzikuta received supplies once every three months from a large shipping truck. On rare occasions when the rough roads were washed out from torrential downpours, large crates of supplies were dropped from a cargo plane.

"Here we go, Sekani!" announced Femi to his son when he saw the general store's owner step out in front.

Sekani rolled his eyes when he saw old man Binah limp forward. He immediately jumped out of the vehicle and headed to the back to open the hatch.

Femi stepped out and stretched his legs.

"Hey, Femi! You heard the news! They're goin' to kill all your stinkin' lions!" he shouted.

"They are not my lions," replied Femi.

"You're betrayin' your own people, Femi. You're a disgrace to your own kind. Shame on you," he said, shaking his head.

Many times Sekani had heard his father try to reason with him, but as usual Binah ignored him; he didn't know if the old man turned a deaf ear to his words or if he was actually hard of hearing.

They walked over to Binah. "Have you received any donations this month?"

"Yeah! All in the back," he hollered. He hobbled over to the front door, turned around with some difficulty, and waited.

Sekani entered the store, and within minutes he was on his way out, carrying a twenty-pound bag of grain over his shoulder.

Femi followed close behind with a ten-gallon jug of water, which he loaded into the jeep.

And Binah hovered near them, breathing down their necks, grunting at them while they worked.

From the corner of his eye, Sekani could see the old man shifting his weight uncomfortably from one leg to the other, growing more impatient by the minute, itching to force his opinion upon them.

"When are you goin' to give up all dis nonsense, Femi?" he spat.

"I'll never understand why you don't see the importance of what I do," Femi said, grabbing the white handkerchief from out of his pants pocket before removing his fedora to wipe the sweat from his forehead.

Binah raised his hand and rubbed his fingers and thumb together. "Got to feed the family," he said, spitting on the ground before looking back at him.

"There are other ways."

Binah looked at the ground and shook his head. His knee buckled under his weight, making him stumble forward.

Sekani rushed to his side.

"Niache!" he shouted, waving his one free arm, dismissively. "Leave me alone! Don't need anybody's help," he said, straightening himself, and then added, "The old man is strong as a water buffalo," he said, pounding his chest with his one free hand.

Sekani threw his hands up in the air and backed away before looking at his father and shrugging.

Femi motioned for him to go back inside.

"I tell ya, you're wastin' your time."

"Whatever it takes for others to see that poaching is wrong! What will you do when the last ivory tusk hits the dry earth? Then what?" he asked, knowing very well that this conversation was a waste of time.

When Sekani had returned, he handed him a case of ammunition, which he loaded onto the backseat of the jeep.

"Are you feedin' all of dis to your boy?" Binah asked.

Femi ignored him.

"Goin' to work with the old man, boy?" he persisted.

"No, I'm taking him to an archaeological camp for the summer," answered Femi.

"Ain't ya a bit old to be playin' in the sand, son? You should be learnin' what real men do."

"A man's worth is measured by the choices he makes in life," said Sekani, heaving a large barrel onto his shoulder.

Tall, dark, and handsome, the sixteen-year-old very much resembled his father.

"You're wasting your time, Sekani," he whispered to his son.

"*Fools!*" Binah cursed.

Femi finished loading up the supplies and slammed the hatch of his jeep shut before walking over to Binah, handing him Kenyan money to pay for the ammunition. When he returned to the jeep, his son was already sitting inside.

The old man hobbled over to them, the sweat gleaming from his forehead. He leaned inside the driver's window. Sekani turned away, trying to avoid smelling the man's foul breath.

"You better keep an eye out for the lions, boy."

Sekani gave old man Binah a quick glance and said, "Yes, sir," before looking away.

The old man slowly backed away, staring at them.

Femi started the engine and pulled away.

"Why do you bother talking to him? You know he will never understand," said Sekani, watching Binah enter the store from his side view mirror.

"Perhaps, but as long as he keeps it up, I'll be reminding him who I am and what I stand for."

CHAPTER 2

NEW BEGINNINGS

The bus bounced over potholes, making the ride very uncomfortable.

"I can't believe I'm in Africa," said Okechuku.

"Neither can I," she muttered, without looking at him. She gazed at the landscape as it flashed by and wondered if all of this was a mistake.

"I can't wait to get to the site. Just imagine what we might find," he said.

Kathleen looked at him, surprised; he seemed excited, not apprehensive like she was.

"Have you ever been to Africa before?" she asked.

"No . . . only on the Discovery Channel." He chuckled. "Have you?"

"No," she said. "This is completely new to me," she mumbled, looking back out the window.

"Hey, don't sweat them! They just don't know how to handle people this cool—not to mention good-looking," he said.

Kathleen looked at him with curiosity and then shook her head and laughed. *Maybe this won't be so bad after all*, she thought.

*   *   *

Sekani looked out of his window, his body swaying back and forth as the jeep bounced over even more potholes.

"Look, Father!"

Femi stopped the jeep. Ten feet away, a black rhinoceros stopped grazing to have a look at the intruders, flicking its ears at the pesky flies before lowering its head, uninterested.

He let the vehicle slowly rolled away for several feet before accelerating. In the distance, a herd of elephants migrated south, possibly heading toward the Tiva River.

They continued northwest for several miles before Femi shifted down to first gear. The jeep descended a steep slope. The rainstorm they had a month ago had washed out the road, leaving the rock bare.

Sekani held on tight to the overhead strap.

Once the road straightened slightly, Femi shifted into second, and then made a sharp turn around a grove of acacia trees before pushing on the clutch and accelerating into third and fourth.

After traveling for over an hour across the savannah, he shifted to four-by-four and began driving carefully through the flooded plains. Back on dry land, they arrived at a narrow road encroached by trees with low bearing branches. Femi downshifted and began a difficult ascent over bare rocks and carved-out soil.

Sekani glanced behind at the supplies; the lighter boxes on top slid to the back window. He grabbed the overhead strap and leaned forward, afraid that the vehicle might tip over.

"We're almost there," Femi said, sensing his son's anxiety.

"I wouldn't want to travel here in a rainstorm," said Sekani, peering out of his window at the washed out road.

Just before reaching the hilltop, the tires skidded on the loose gravel, jolting the vehicle to one side. Sekani gasped, tightening his grip on the overhead strap. He sighed when they finally made it over the bare rock onto the flat plain.

Femi stopped the vehicle and stepped out to survey the steep cliff they had just climbed. Sekani followed.

"Do we have to take the same road back?" Sekani asked.

"No, there's another way, but it would take a bit longer. From here we will have to head north in order to meet with the road before heading south," he explained. "Well, then, let's go. We're only half an hour away, and I wanted to get you to the site before nightfall."

Sekani checked his watch. They should be arriving at the Moja tribal grounds by noon.

The road slithered north through green plains of tall grass, interlaced with groves of trees and thickets and the occasional detour around fallen trees. As they continued, the landscape gradually transformed into a jungle. They turned left onto a narrow path and drove for another twenty minutes until they passed two large statues of a warrior standing back to back with a lion holding a spear in its forepaws erected on either side of the road.

"That's new!" commented Femi.

As soon as they entered the threshold, children appeared from the forest, running toward them, jumping and shouting with excitement. The seemingly quiet, primitive village was now boisterous and lively.

"I love coming here; no other place makes you feel more welcome or appreciated," Femi said, laughing.

Sekani smiled.

They opened the doors carefully and were immediately greeted by a mob of smiling boys and girls, eagerly extending their hands through the crowd to touch the visitors.

One by one, Femi and Sekani grabbed the children's hands; their excited voices resonated throughout the small village.

Femi walked to the back of the jeep and opened the hatch.

Sekani smiled; their tiny faces lit up when his father started to hand out granola bars, chips, and chocolates.

Senior Elder Gatimu approached Femi, giving him one of his toothless smiles. He grabbed both of his hands, greeting him.

"*Shikamoo*," said Femi.

"*Shikamoo*," replied Gatimu.

Femi followed the senior elder into his home, leaving Sekani to unload the freshwater, food, supplies, and clothing. It wasn't long before Sekani had all the help he needed. Children of all ages lined up to create a long chain. They passed down supplies, hands over head, skipping over the younger and shorter of the helpers, their constant chatter buzzing in the village while they worked. Several times, the older children stopped to give their younger siblings a chance to help, loading their arms with lighter supplies before continuing; the young ones jubilantly accepted their load and ran away, dropping the supplies in a pile by a tree before eagerly returning for more.

After they had emptied the jeep, the boys came up to Sekani and began questioning him.

"*Una miaka mingapi?*" One boy called out. Though Sekani understood the language, he didn't feel comfortable speaking it, even though he had lived in Africa most of his life.

"I'm sixteen," he answered.

"*Una mpenzi?*" Another shouted.

Sekani chuckled. "No, I don't have a girlfriend."

The girls huddled at the treeline, giggling.

"*Unahudhuria shule?*"

"Yes, I go to school. I'm in grade eleven."

"*Unapenda michezo?*"

"Yes, I do love sports. I'm training to be a runner."

"*Kukimbia?*" Several children shouted and laughed.

"Yeah! Kukimbia. To be faster . . . maybe for the Olympics," he said with pride.

"Oooooooooh!" The children chortled.

Sekani saw his father exit the thatched cabin with the senior elder.

"I see you have some admirers," commented Femi when he saw a group of boys standing beside him. The girls stood in the distance, their bright smiles flashing at him.

"Yeah! I guess so." He smiled at them.

Once in the jeep, Femi started to shift into reverse when he noticed Senior Elder Gatimu walking toward them. He walked with difficulty, leaning most of his weight on an old piece of driftwood. Femi wondered why he wasn't using the cane he had brought him last year.

"For you and your boy," he said, handing them two identical necklaces made out of animal teeth and bones. "To keep the *roho mbaya* away," he added before backing away.

Femi thanked him, shifted into reverse, pulling away carefully so as to not run over any children, and then began to drive down the well-beaten path. In the rearview mirror, he saw the children running after their vehicle. At the threshold, the children stopped and waved. A row of white stones had been neatly placed around the perimeter.

"What are those for?" asked Sekani.

"They reflect the moonlight to ward off evil spirits."

Femi extended his hand out the window and waved. Sekani did the same.

"What did he mean about keeping the evil spirit away?" asked Sekani while he examined his necklace: a row of canine teeth in black metal clasps, separated by small bone fragments hung on a string. He wondered if the teeth were that of a lion.

"The Moja tribe, like many other tribes, have their beliefs and superstitions. They believe that the evil spirit, or *roho mbaya*, as he called it, has something to do with the disappearance of children," he explained.

"Children? I didn't hear that on the news."

"It makes me wonder how much more is going on that we don't hear about. Many of the villages are so secluded and remote that if something were to happen to them, the outside world would never know about it.

"Apparently, a child has gone missing from a small village, ten miles east of here, but there's something else."

"What?"

"Senior Elder Gatimu kept saying 'beware of the *Mashujaa Wa Mchanga*,' and something about them rising to fight once again."

"Again! Is he referring to the Mchanga-Misitu War?"

"Yeah!"

"Didn't the war happen, like, two thousand years ago?" asked Sekani.

"I believe so."

"Who won?"

"That's just it. No one knows. Everyone just . . . vanished," Femi explained.

Sekani slipped the necklace on. "Not bad."

"You make anything look good, son," said Femi, ruffling Sekani's hair.

CHAPTER 3

TSAVO ARCHAEOLOGICAL SITE

As requested by Sekani, they avoided traveling back on the same washed-out road and headed north to connect with another dirt road, which would lead them south toward Tsavo East National Park.

Three hours later, they passed through the west gates of South Kitui National Reserve, crossed the arid savannah, and arrived at the park.

In the distance, scattered trees provided limited shade for a pride of lions.

Femi spotted a large truck with a canvas cab parked several kilometres away from the road, near the lions.

"Let's check it out," he said.

At this rate, we'll never get to the site before nightfall, thought Sekani.

His father knew every tour bus and vehicle that entered the park, but this was one he wasn't familiar with. He was protective of the wildlife, and he was probably wondering who they were and what they were doing positioned so close to the pride.

He turned off the road and drove slowly toward the truck. As they approached, Sekani saw a tall, white, scrawny man standing in front of the parked vehicle. The man removed his glasses before leaning over to peer through his telephoto lens.

Another man peeked from behind the truck and tapped on the canvas cab twice before taking a few steps toward them, stopping to watch, a look of concern on his face.

A woman with a large, brimmed hat stepped out, taking care to not trip on the narrow steps as she descended. She moved elegantly, her face hidden behind her hat, and her ebony skin was in beautiful contrast to her white long-sleeved blouse. The woman stepped closer, peered from beneath the hat, and smiled.

"Well, I'll be darned," said Femi, turning off the engine. He jumped out of the jeep and stood, staring at her.

Her concerned expression soon changed to one of recognition and excitement.

"Femi!" she called out, flashing her perfect white teeth.

"Hanna!" he replied. They caressed and then pulled away from each other, holding hands before giving each other another embrace.

"How long has it been?" she asked.

"At least five years," he said. Sekani could tell that his father was blushing and smiled.

Femi looked at Sekani.

"I want you to meet someone," he said, walking over to him. Sekani stepped out of the jeep and smiled.

"Is that who I think it is?" she said, shifting her attention from Femi to Sekani. "Hi, Sekani!"

"Hi!"

"Have you ever grown! I remember when you were just a little boy," she said. She spoke articulately with a slight exotic accent. "He looks just like you, but I do see a bit of Sandra in him," she said to Femi.

Sekani studied his father at the mention of his mother's name. He knew his father didn't feel comfortable talking about her.

Femi glanced at Sekani and gave him a forced smile.

"How have you been doing?" she asked Femi, grabbing his hand as if their last meeting had been only yesterday. Femi guided her to the front of her truck.

"I'm good!"

"Have you been able to let go of her?" she asked.

"You were never one to beat around the bush," Femi said, taking his fedora off to wipe the sweat off his face while thinking of ways to change the subject.

"I saw that you flinched at the sound of her name," she insisted.

Femi stared into the distance and donned his hat before clearing his throat. She grabbed his arm gently. He looked at her and knew better than to avoid answering her.

"It's been hard, but I've been coping,"

"Well, you've done an amazing job raising Sekani on your own."

Femi glanced at Sekani, who was now sitting in the jeep, and smirked while nodding to himself. He straightened himself and watched the two men studying the lions.

"How's the pride?" asked Femi, feeling that it was now safe to change the subject. He hoped that she would drop the conversation about Sandra.

"Well . . . I don't know. We lost a lioness just last week . . . I still haven't found her. I can't seem to get any transmission from her collar. I fear that she was killed or taken away," she explained.

"Why?"

"The lioness was young and healthy. I don't know what could have happened to her."

"I haven't seen any activity in the region," he said.

Hanna looked towards her teammates, who were now engaged in a heavy discussion.

"Have you noticed anything different in their behaviour?" asked Femi.

"Ah! They're always fighting . . . just like an old married couple, these two." She gave him a big smile.

Femi shook his head and chuckled.

"Oh!" she cried. "You mean the lions. Well, if you are insinuating that these lions are responsible for the deaths, and now . . . disappearances . . ." Hanna shook her head. "Not a chance."

"Tell you what. I'm taking Sekani to the Tsavo Archaeological Site. After I've dropped him off, I'll take a drive around to see if I can spot your missing lioness."

"Would you? Thank you, Femi," she said, stepping on her tiptoes and kissing him on the cheek. On their way back to the jeep, Femi saw Sekani slouched down in the front seat, his feet sticking out of the window, listening to music on his iPod.

"Nice to see you again, Sekani," Hanna said before turning away to join her teammates.

Femi cleared his throat and waited for a brief second before knocking Sekani's feet from off the window and yanked his earphones out of his ears.

"What?" Sekani bolted up, surprised.

Femi glowered at him.

"It was nice to meet you!" he shouted after Hanna, who glanced back and waved at them.

Femi climbed inside, turned the key, and watched them, lost in his thoughts.

"So why haven't you dated her, Father?" asked Sekani.

"Oh! What would she possibly see in a guy like me? Besides, I'm too busy," said Femi, shifting the jeep into gear.

"Right! Mother died eleven years ago. You should find a better excuse . . . besides, you like her, and she likes you."

"Yeah, yeah!" He paused. "Do you really think she likes me?"

"It couldn't be more obvious. I don't know what you're waiting for, but if I were you, I . . ."

"You would what?" he asked, scowling at him

"I . . . I would ask her out," said Sekani, avoiding his glare and hiding the smirk stretched across his face.

"Yeah!" he muttered under his breath and sighed.

Sekani glanced at his father; he knew he liked Hanna very much, and understood that the thought of losing someone again was too unbearable for him. He wondered if he would ever let go. He was a good man and deserved more.

They drove in silence until Sekani saw the site flash by.

"Father? Father, are you all right?" he shouted.

"What?" he said.

"You drove right past it?"

He made a U-turn, drove back, and slammed on the brakes, burying everything, including them, in a cloud of red dust.

"This is it!" he said, glancing over his shoulder. Sekani leaned over to have a look.

A throng of teens sauntered about, setting up camp and talking to each other.

To the left, beyond a large wooden sign with the faded words "Tsavo Archaeological Site," rows of tents and shelter boxes were pitched in the sand.

On the right, nestled against Babu Mountain, a large white linen cloth, draped securely over a steady wooden-framed structure, sheltered a long rectangular table. At either end, a screen kept unwanted insects from entering.

Sekani's eyes drifted to a gorgeous blonde who was leaning back, her eyes closed, seemingly enjoying the hot sun on her fair skin. She shook her thick mane of long hair, occasionally glancing over to the plump boy sitting beside her, talking.

His father followed Sekani's gaze.

"Now that's not a sight you often see in Africa, is it?"

"Yeah!" he said dreamily.

"Well, you can always change your mind about staying here," Femi said.

"Nope, I think this was a great idea, Father. Didn't you say that this camp would be a great learning experience and a chance to make new friends?" he said, smiling at his father, who seemed to be regretting his decision.

Sekani stepped out of the jeep, opened the hatchback, and grabbed his backpack, tent, and sleeping bag before slamming the door. He walked over to his father's window.

"You could always come to work with me. I'll even let you carry a Winchester," his father said, trying to entice Sekani.

Sekani laughed aloud, making several teens look in his direction. "So you trust me more with a rifle than around a pretty girl," he teased.

"Yeah! You can say that." Femi said, trying to keep a straight face. "Oh! All right! Professor Holdsworth is a good friend of mine and is very trustworthy," he added, grabbing his hand and giving him an affectionate one-arm hug.

"Don't worry! I'll see you when you drop by," Sekani said before walking away.

"Sure thing, probably in four or five days. Have fun, and take care of yourself!" he shouted after him.

"I will," he replied, giving him a small wave.

He turned around and saw a thin older man in a white T-shirt and cargo shorts walk over to him. He removed his hat and scratched his head. "Professor Holdsworth," he introduced himself and then gazed at the cloud of dust swirling behind Sekani's father's jeep as he drove away. "Your dad is a good man. He helped me get this camp established. He knows a lot of people . . . very well liked. Let me take you on a tour," he said.

"This is our bulletin board, where we post the activity of the day or any important messages we may have," he explained.

"Here is the wash station." He pointed to a large portable sink with a soap dispenser. A large, heavy-duty plastic drum containing water and supported by a solid wooden frame towered over them.

"Here is our dining area." They walked past the large structure he had seen earlier and stopped in front of two smaller tents adjacent to the dining area. "And this is where your meals will be prepared. Should anyone need medical attention, we have a nursing station here as well."

They crossed the site, walking to where rows of tents and shelter boxes were pitched.

"You know the language. Where would you pitch your tent?" asked the professor.

Sekani saw two signs at the head of the sleeping quarters: *msichana* for girl and *mvulana* for boy.

"I think I will set up my tent with the *msichana*." The professor raised an eyebrow.

"Just kidding, Professor," said Sekani.

"Good! Hope you enjoy your stay," he said, patting him on the shoulder before walking away.

Two girls stood nearby, gawking at him, occasionally pulling away from their stare to whisper to each other.

Sekani pulled out his nylon tent from its casing, unrolled it, and began spreading it over the soil.

"I hope you have a ground sheet sewn in the floor of your tent." He looked up and saw that the girls who had been staring at him had joined him.

"I'm Lisha," said one of the girls. She wore long-sleeved blouse and light-coloured pants; her dark complexion and eyes radiated a natural beauty, and her smile was genuine.

"Hi!" he replied, straightening himself.

"Do you need help with setting up?" asked the other girl, who also wore her hair short, but was less conservative in what she wore, and her smile seemed to suggest that she was very much aware of her beauty. "I'm Tanisha," she said flirtatiously.

"No, thanks. I'm all right."

"Okay, if you need anything, just ask," they said before walking away, glancing back at him several times and giggling.

After he had finished pitching his tent, he stood up and scanned the site when his eyes met hers—the white girl with the long blonde hair. Sekani smiled and waved, sheepishly. The girl gave him a small smile and looked away.

Definitely have to get to know her, he thought.

"All right! Everyone . . . listen up . . . come now!" shouted the professor. He waited until he had everyone's attention before proceeding.

"My name is Adrian Holdsworth. I'm a professor of archaeology from the University of Western Ontario in Canada. I would like to welcome you to the Tsavo Archaeological Site!" shouted the professor. "Before I introduce you to the team, I have a few important announcements to make.

"This camp runs for the month of August, and it's a very long time, should you not get along with one another. So I'm asking you to leave your cultural differences behind and take the opportunity to get to know one another. Our goal is to learn from each other and to build friendships that perhaps will last a lifetime.

"Now, most of you are from this region, but there are a few amongst you for whom this visit to Africa is their first. Though this country is beautiful, it can also be quite harsh, dangerous, and unforgiving. That is why I cannot emphasize enough how important it is to stay together.

"We will implement a buddy system. Once you have been designated to a team, I want you to pick a buddy. If you happen to be in a team of three, you will all be buddies to one another.

"Another important rule: Remember to keep your tent closed at all times—otherwise, you will be in for a nasty surprise. And no one maybe in closed quarters with a person of the opposite sex, at any time. If you must speak to someone of the opposite sex, you must do it in the open."

Chuckles resonated from the crowd.

"I hope I make myself clear. Should any of you disobey this rule, you will be joining the kitchen crew. Don't take this punishment lightly: you will see firsthand how it feels to cook in this heat.

"Now, I will introduce you to our crew who will be assisting you during your stay: Michelle Standfort, our coordinator; Sade Sakala, our translator; Dr. Iris Racine, our physician; and last but not least, our kitchen/comfort crew, Lucas, Moses, Leticia, and Tsimba.

"I would introduce you to Dr. Matheson Blackwell, our anthropologist, but she's away on call and perhaps will be joining us later.

"I believe I have everyone's completed application forms with me. Anyone who has food allergies and has not completed section C of the form, please see Dr. Racine.

"I would like for all of you to treat our servers with the utmost respect and courtesy.

"All right! Now that you have met everyone, here's a little history lesson," announced the professor.

The majority of the group booed and moaned, while others stood silently, shifting from one foot to the other, signalling their impatience and boredom. The crew disappeared into their respective tents, while Mrs. Standfort stayed for the lesson.

"Tsavo National Park is one of the largest and oldest parks in Kenya. A railway divides the park into east and west. We will be working in the east, where the arid soil gives us the perfect conditions for excavating. What you will mostly find are arrowheads, tools, and clay pots dating back to the Stone Age.

"These cliffs here," he said, pointing to Babu Mountain, "were used as rock shelters, where many of the clans lived.

"Since it's getting late, we will be establishing your teams. Tomorrow, you will select the area your team will excavate. These yellow wooden stakes mark where we will be digging." He extended his hand to a small, cleared patch of land, where the shade provided by Babu Mountain stretched over part of the designated area.

Mrs. Standfort would like to say a few words," he announced. A thin, white woman wearing khaki shorts and matching T-shirt stepped forward. Her short, dark hair accentuated her green eyes.

"Every morning, I will put your team's agenda on zis board," she said, pointing at the bulletin board. Everyone strained to listen to what she had to say, for she spoke softly, mesmerizing many of the boys with her French European accent. "While our preliminary reason for being 'ere is archaeology, we will organize field trips for you, so zat you may experience a wide spectrum of activity.

"Now, let's find out which teams you belong to.

"Okay, team one: Kat'leen? Is Kat'leen 'ere?" Mrs. Standfort called out.

The white girl with the long, blonde hair looked up. "Yeah! I'm here."

Sekani looked up and made a mental note of her name.

"You will be joining Kianga and Okechuku in team one," she said, drawing the number one in the sand.

"Team two: Chase, Adesina, Sekani, and Lisha. Please line up over 'ere.

"Team t'ree: Amber, Sadia, Tanisha, and Joseph. You guys will be over 'ere.

"Now that you know who's on your team, I want you to get to know each odder's name. I also want you to give your team a name.

Ze name must be African in origin and must be somet'ing we find in the savannah.

"Ze one wit' ze most unusual name will win a prize. Ze next challenge will be posted on ze board, tomorrow.

"On tonight's agenda, we will meet at ze fire pit. T'ere we'll be 'ot dogs and marshmallows.

I 'ope you enjoy your stay. I look forward to working wit' all of you. See you all tonight," she concluded before walking away.

Once she finished speaking, the conversation between members started.

"That's kind of ironic," said Okechuku, glancing at the other teams.

"What's ironic?" asked Kathleen.

"Just how we met, and now we are on the same team."

Kathleen looked at him for a brief moment in disbelief before she searched the crowd.

"Who are you looking for?" he asked, when he noticed she was preoccupied with something else.

"Haven't you noticed, O—sorry, how do you say your name?"

"Just call me Oke."

"All right, Oke! Haven't you noticed that we are missing a team member?"

Okechuku looked around.

The professor must have noticed they were searching for someone when he approached them. "You're missing Kianga," Professor Holdsworth said, turning around. He took a large sidestep away from the crowd to get a better look past the group of teens. He spotted a girl sitting on a rock in the distance. "*Kianga!*" he shouted. He motioned for her to come before walking away.

The black girl who had been rude to her on the bus stood up and slowly walked toward them.

"Great!" Kathleen mumbled.

"What was that, Buttercup?" she asked, slamming her shoulder into hers, shoving her aside.

"Hey, watch it!" shouted Kathleen, rubbing her shoulder.

"Shut up, *Mzungu.*"

Kathleen turned to Okechuku. "What does that mean?" she whispered to him.

"I think it means 'white person.'"

"Oh!"

CHAPTER 4

FABLE OF THE CURSED WARRIORS

Kathleen sat on the red soil, leaned back on her elbows, and closed her eyes, embracing the sun's warmth while she listened to Okechuku.

"So where are you from?" he asked.

"Strange enough, I'm from the same city as the professor," she responded, without as much as a glance.

"Small world! I'm from New Orleans. My parents thought it would be a good idea to get me off the couch." He shook his belly. "They knew someone from work who had their kids go to an archaeological camp, and they loved it."

"Who? The kids or the parents?" remarked Kianga.

"I think it was taught by the same professor," added Okechuku, ignoring Kianga's comment.

"And what about you, Kianga? Where are you from?" asked Kathleen.

"None of your business," she snapped while carving a stick with her jackknife. Her tightly braided rows of hair, gathered together with one yellow ribbon, were in direct contrast to her tattered jeans and tank top.

"Looks like we are going to have a great time," said Kathleen, rolling her eyes.

"Do you have a problem?" she said, pausing from her whittling to stare Kathleen down.

"Yeah! I do, and I'm staring at her," she said, standing up to face her.

"Oh, relax, Buttercup!" she said dismissively. "You're no match for me," she concluded before returning to her carving.

Okechuku and Kathleen looked at each other and shrugged their shoulders.

Kathleen sat back down beside Okechuku, feeling humiliation's sting. She closed her eyes and tried to dismiss Kianga's comments. *Who does she think she is?* she thought. *And I could have sworn I saw her smile. Was she finding this amusing?*

Kathleen may have been brought up in the perfect home in the perfect neighbourhood, but the Gallant family name was known for having strong values and for standing up for what they believed. She decided to let it go, for now, knowing her time would come.

Kathleen pulled out an elastic from her pocket and combed her hair with her fingers, untangling the knots before gathering all her hair into a ponytail.

"Did your parents send you here, too?" asked Okechuku.

"Well, sort of . . . my dad came over on business. He's overseeing a telecommunications project in Nairobi. So my parents thought it would be educational for me to come here. What do your parents do?" asked Kathleen.

"My mom stays at home with my four brothers. My dad is one of the captains who navigate the stern-wheel steamboat on the Mississippi River. Did you know that the river is the second-longest river system in the United States? And it is the largest in North America. It so interchangeable, you have to know it like the back of your hand. But it's too much for one person to learn it all. So every captain has a designated section of the river to navigate. To get the job you have to memorize the river's embankment and be able to map the area with your eyes closed."

"I've never heard of that type of job before. Sounds interesting!"

"Yeah, he loves it. He first started as a deckhand when he was fifteen years old, painting and maintaining the boat, but he watched others and learned. One day, a situation arose where the pilot on shift was injured, and my dad took control and piloted the steamboat safely. The captain was impressed; he made him first mate before teaching him everything he needed to know to become a pilot. Seventeen years later, he was promoted to captain."

"That's sick!" she said.

"Kianga, what do your parents do?" asked Okechuku.

"You're assuming I *have* parents," she answered, without so much as raising an eyebrow from her whittling.

"Okay, kids! Tomorrow morning you'll reveal your team's name and choose your site for excavating. Now dinner is ready. Please clean up at the washing station," announced Professor Holdsworth.

"Mmm! Mmm! I sure love food," remarked Okechuku.

"I would never have guessed," said Kianga as she headed towards the crowd that was gathering around the portable sink.

"What's her problem? Don't pay any attention to her," Kathleen said.

Okechuku smiled.

"No worries. I'm used to it," he replied. "She's insecure with her looks. Poor girl!"

Kathleen laughed. A sense of relief overcame her, for she was content he was on her team.

Once seated under the white canopy, Kathleen couldn't believe how much cooler it felt in the shade. A nice breeze flowed through the dining area, rippling the draped walls.

She glanced at Kianga, who was shoving food into her mouth, oblivious to everyone having stopped to stare at her.

Kianga raised her eyes and stopped chewing when she realized that everyone was watching her. She pushed her half-finished plate of food away, got up, and walked out.

Soon the chatter of students, busily exchanging stories about their lives, filled the air.

Kathleen stared at her plate and waited. She didn't know where to start.

"Are you going to eat anything?" asked Okechuku.

Kathleen sat silently.

"This is *ugali*. It's made with maize flour and water. You use it to scoop up your stew . . . like you would with bread. This green stuff is *sukuma wiki*, which is kale, and here is grilled *nyama choma*, which is goat meat cooked with onions and tomatoes," explained Okechuku. "Do you want to know how it's prepared?"

"I'd rather not," she smiled. "Where did you learn all of this?"

"From the Internet and the Food Network."

"Do you want to be a chef, Oke?" she asked.

"How did you know?"

"I just know these things," she answered. They both laughed.

One of the cooks came by and asked her if she would prefer something else. Kathleen smiled and declined. She didn't want to be impolite; besides, she came here for the experience and wasn't going to miss out on anything.

She grabbed a piece of *ugali*, scooped the stew, and took a mouthful. Her eyes immediately lit up. "This is good," she said to Okechuku. She glanced up and saw the cook anxiously watching her.

Pleased by her reaction, the cook walked away, content.

Okechuku laughed.

Kathleen's eyes drifted to the teen she'd seen earlier; he had been watching her. He smiled at her. Embarrassed, she went back to eating.

*   *   *

After dropping Sekani off, Femi decided to head back to where Hanna was stationed. On the way, he radioed the dispatcher for Tsavo National Park to ask him if any of the game wardens had seen a lioness wearing a tracking collar. The dispatcher confirmed that no lions with a radio collar had been found or seen.

As the jeep bounced over the rough terrain, he reached for his cell phone and called the operator.

"Can you put me through to the Nairobi Police Department?" he asked. The line went quiet for a moment before he heard a pulsating ring on the other end. A woman's voice answered.

"Nairobi Police Department! How may I direct your call?"

"Is Constable Whitmore available? You can let him know that it's Femi Kaita." He decided to switch to hands-free mode while he waited. After a short pause, a familiar voice boomed in the speaker, startling him.

"Femi Kaita? Son of Romani and Adia Kaita? Well, how have you been?"

"Good! Can't complain!"

"You can, but what's the point. No one's gonna listen to ya anyway, I say," he said, his loud, hearty laugh drowning out the sound of the engine.

"Yeah!" he said, smiling and nodding.

"I've heard that you're working as a game warden for the Tsavo National Park."

"You heard right."

"Just like the old man, ain't ya? Don't like being tied down to a desk. Nothing better than to roam the outbacks. How's the old man, still enjoying retirement?"

"He sure is. He's been working hard ever since."

Constable Whitmore laughed so hard that he started coughing. After a few moments he continued. "Isn't that the way?" He paused, cleared his throat, and asked, "I'm sure you're not just callin' to chat with the old man. What's on your mind, son?"

"I need to get the coroner's report on these lion attacks. Is that something you can help me with?"

Silence. The groaning sound of the jeep made it difficult to hear. Femi turned up the volume.

"Are you still there, Constable?"

"Yeah! Yeah! I'm here! Why do you need to see those, son?"

"Just trying to make sense of it all . . . maybe reading the reports would shed some light on what's happening."

"I'll tell you what's happening, son. It's just a sign of the times, you know . . . The human population is growing and taking up their land. It's just their way of fighting back."

"That might be the case, but I still need to look into it," Femi said, even though he didn't agree with the constable's explanation. After a long pause, he added, "Have to make sure I've looked at everything. The top guys want a thorough analysis, not just a fancy report with theories and speculations . . . They want answers, if you know what I mean." He hoped that would persuade him.

"I sure understand ya! Always someone breathing down your neck and ready to point fingers if you're wrong. Well, I would usually say no, but since your dad is a great friend of mine . . ." he said.

There was a short pause before Femi finally heard what he wanted.

"Okay. I'll see what I can do."

"Can you fax it to me at the Kanzikuta General Store, when you get them?"

"Sure will, Femi. Whenever you're in Nairobi, don't forget to pay the old man a visit, and tell your dad to not be a stranger."

"I will! Thanks!" Femi said.

He switched the phone off.

In the distance, a black dot in a field of sun-scorched grass caught his attention. The stifling heat created a haze, making it difficult to focus ahead. He turned off the main road and started toward it. He soon realized that he'd found Hanna and her crew; they had moved from their previous location. Femi stopped the jeep.

Her teammates glanced up to look at him while Hanna remained crouched on the ground, examining something in the grass.

Femi jumped out of his vehicle.

"What did you find there?" he said.

"Hi!" replied a tall man.

"Hello!" said the shorter of the two, glancing up at Femi before running to their truck. He quickly returned carrying a black bag and handed it to Hanna. Femi squatted down beside her.

"What do you make of this?" said Femi, covering his nose with his handkerchief. The stench from the half-decomposed carcass nauseated him.

She straightened herself before wiping her forehead with the back of her sleeve.

"Well, it's our lioness," Hanna said.

"How do you know?" asked Femi.

"This is one of our radio collars," she explained, pointing at the bloodstained collar lying on the grass several feet away.

"Do you know what might have done this to her?"

"Looks like she was attacked, but why? That's what I want to know." She opened the bag, grabbed some vials, and began removing tissue samples from the body. After she gave the dead animal a thorough examination, she removed her gloves and began recording her findings on a small voice recorder.

"Laceration of the upper leg and hip suggests . . ." Hanna walked away while speaking into her recorder.

"My name is Lee."

"Hunter."

Crouched on the ground, Femi shook their hands.

"Femi," he said, standing up while looking in the distance, followed by the others.

"We've heard all about you, Femi," said Lee. He removed his glasses, cleaning the lenses with the tail of his T-shirt before putting them back on.

"All good, I hope."

"Yep! She really likes you," continued Lee.

Femi cleared his throat and changed the subject. "It's too bad about the lioness."

"Yeah. Well, we better bag her and take her to the lab," said Hunter, tossing a pair of latex gloves to Lee before putting a pair on himself.

"What could have done this?" asked Femi.

"Isn't it obvious?" said Hanna, who had just returned. "Look at the caudal vertebrae . . . completely crushed, and the cervical vertebrae." She pointed to its mangled neck. "Crushed as well. I can only think of one animal that has the power to pulverize bones like this," she said while assisting Hunter and Lee in recovering the carcass and placing it in the bag.

"A hyena," said Femi.

"Precisely," she agreed, looking up at Femi.

Even while she was sweating and panting, she truly looked beautiful, he thought.

"But hyenas are scavengers," he commented.

"Yes, but they have been known to be successful in hunting as a pack," Lee remarked.

"Why would they leave the carcass?" asked Hunter.

"I don't know. I did a thorough examination, and there are no other indications that she was killed by anything else. I have to get to our lab and run some tests. The samples should confirm my findings," explained Hanna. "I don't understand why she wasn't eaten by the hyenas. Doesn't make any sense!"

"I agree. Well, I'll be getting out of your way," said Femi. "I'll catch you at another time. Nice meeting you." He waved at Lee and Hunter and walked away.

He watched them from inside the jeep. He had hoped to ask her out on a date, but he didn't feel the timing was appropriate. He also felt betrayed by a sudden wave of anxiety. He definitely wasn't ready for this. He started the engine and began driving off when he saw Hanna wave at him.

"Femi!" she shouted, running over to him and panting.

"Safari is an hour away from the lab. Do you want to grab a bite?" she asked.

"Are you sure? I mean . . ."

"Yeah! I'm fine. I'm sad about it, but it would be nice to get away from it all," she said. "Besides, we have lots to catch up on," she added with a smile.

"Oh, I just remembered I have to be somewhere . . ." he said, jokingly. He gave her a small sigh before agreeing, "Oh! All right! What time?"

"Around eight. I'll meet you there."

"Sounds good! See you then," he said.

She leaned inside the window and kissed him on the cheek before returning to Lee and Hunter, who had been watching like two high school girls; Hanna quickly motioned for them to get back to work.

Femi started the engine. *Isn't it funny how some things just have a way of working out?* A strange sentiment overwhelmed him, something he hadn't felt in a long time—happiness. Though he was content with his life and Sekani, something had been missing.

*   *   *

Surprised by how cold it could get in Africa, Kathleen was grateful that her mother had packed a couple of warm sweaters, sweatshirts, jeans, socks, and a warm fleece blanket.

After ensuring that her tent was tightly sealed, Kathleen walked over to the fire, where Okechuku was anxiously waiting for her to join him. She quickly sat down in the chair he had saved for her and wrapped herself in a blanket.

In the distance, crickets chirped loudly. Darkness had fallen, leaving them clinging to the warmth and light from the fire.

Kathleen held her flashlight tightly against her body. She glanced over her shoulders, unable to see beyond the orange glow the fire was emitting. A wall of darkness surrounded them. She shuddered at the thought of what could be lurking in the tall grass. She returned her gaze to the fire, smiling nervously at Okechuku. Kathleen shuddered again.

"Are you all right?" Okechuku whispered to her.

"Yeah!" she nodded, a slight shiver creeping under her skin.

Okechuku looked at her sternly.

"No, really, I'm fine," she added before shifting her attention to what the others were saying, trying hard to not be frightened.

Stories, legends, and tall tales circled the fire as each veteran camper eagerly participated, trying hard to scare the newcomers. Besides Amber, Chase, and her, they were the only white teenagers attending the Archaeological Camp—which the others greatly took advantage of.

"Do you have a story for us, Lisha?" asked the professor.

Lisha nervously looked around at the crowd before shaking her head.

Kathleen rolled her eyes at Lisha's exaggerated efforts to scare them.

"Do you remember a tale, perhaps one your parents told you when you were younger?"

"I do know of a tale, but . . ." she stopped and shook her head, again.

"Ah! Come on!" shouted several of her friends.

"She don't know anything," said her younger brother, Joseph.

"No . . . I know of one, but I don't t'ink you can take it," said Lisha, glowering at Joseph. "I mean, it's a true story and all, but I don't t'ink the *Mzungu* will be able to 'andle it," she added. Her thick African accent gave the story the perfect ambiance.

"That's not nice, Lisha," corrected the professor.

"Sorry," she said, glancing at Kathleen, who shrugged her shoulders as to say she wasn't offended by her comment.

"Stop bluffing, Lisha," shouted Okechuku, who seemed to be enjoying the lead-in to her story. Kathleen looked at him, surprised, before smiling.

The light from the fire twinkled in everyone's eyes, except for Kianga, who sat a few feet away from the circle with her head down, looking downright miserable.

Across from her, she could tell that the teen from earlier had been watching her. Several times her eyes drifted over the flames toward him, only to meet his. Embarrassed, she quickly looked away. She glanced at him again and saw that he was now paying close attention to Lisha.

"Okay . . . I'll tell you, but don't say I didn't warn ya." she continued. With one hand on her hip and the other held in front of her, she waved her little finger in the air, taking the time to look at every glowing face before starting.

What an act, thought Kathleen.

"T'ousands of years ago, t'ere was two kingdoms, *Mashujaa Wa Mchanga* and *Walinzi Wa Misitu*. The Mchanga tribe, for short, which was protected by t'is very mountain," pointing to the dark silhouette of Babu Mountain behind her, "was ruled by King Hundo. He was a great leader, powerful but fair. He looked out for 'is people.

"But to the west, on the Atlantic Coast, t'ere was an enchanted forest, known by all as Milele. Milele means *forever* for all of you who don't know; it is a story about a beautiful girl who . . ."

"Stick with the first story, sis!" shouted Joseph.

"Oh! All right! Maybe later . . . Milele provided the tribes with all the food, shelter, medicine, and all the t'ings they needed to live a 'ealthy and 'appy life, but t'ere was an important rule that they must abide by: No one can stay. They're to keep moving and not claim the land as their own.

"Tribes from all around followed this rule until Misitu tribe's king died. The new king, King Rapula, was a 'arsh man. He did not listen to the rules. He ordered his people to stay and claim the forest as theirs, defending it against whoever would wander near. Many wars broke out, but the king and his army were too powerful. And his people were too frightened to leave. If they tried to leave, he would cut off t'eir heads and t'rust them 'igh into the air, on spikes and spears, as a warning to ot'ers."

"That's horrible," said Amber.

"It gets worse," she continued. "Milele was dyin'. The freshwater springs dried up, trees and plants died, and animals disappeared. The land had been stripped away.

"The people of Misitu were starting to die, but the king and his army continued, marchin' into nearby villages, takin' the men and women and killin' the elders and the children.

"But one day the king died, and his heir, Kokayi, took the t'rone. He led his people east t'rough the 'ot, dry desert, traveling for months until they arrived to the kingdom of Mchanga. Kokayi promised his people, weak with fatigue, famine, and disease, a better life. They made a shelter for the women and children who survived the journey, and led the men and boys to the Mchanga's guarded fortress. Under the cover of night, the Misitu men attacked.

"But Hundo was no fool. To Kokayi's surprise, the king and his army defended it well. They waited for the attackers to enter deep into the village before flankin' them on all sides and forcin' Kokayi and his men to surrender.

"Legend says that a wanderin' traveller found the city deserted with no one in sight. Everyone had disappeared," concluded Lisha.

"If everyone disappeared, how is it that we know Kokayi surrendered?" asked Okechuku.

"You make a good point," affirmed Sekani.

"Thanks," said Okechuku.

Sekani smiled at him and then looked at Kathleen.

"I heard of that. They say that the warriors' ghosts still roam the land," said Adesina.

"There are no such things as ghosts," said Chase, dismissively.

"My family believes that the ghosts of lost ones walk the land of the living as long as there is someone to remember him or her. Once that generation is gone, the ghost moves on," explained Tanisha.

"Some say that the warriors from both kingdoms, including the women and children, turned to dust, while others believe that the Mchanga's army was cursed to roam the night as lions, and the Misitu army as hyenas—which would explain the animosity between the lions and hyenas," said Sekani. His deep voice resonated in the night. Sekani looked again at Kathleen, who, in turn, glanced away.

Everyone sat silently, lost in thought. The wind rustled the grass, and a loud cackle from a hyena nearby broke the silence. Kathleen and Okechuku jumped out of their chairs while others looked startled.

The professor stood up and flashed his light into the darkness. Red eyes danced in the distance.

"That was creepy!" said Okechuku.

"That might be him listening to us," said Amber.

"Whatever," muttered Kianga as she pulled her chair closer to the group.

Kathleen couldn't help but smile.

*   *   *

She walked barefoot towards a tree; its twisted trunk resembled two pythons, wrapped in a tight embrace. Low bearing branches armed with thorns stretched out like claws, waiting to ensnare anything or anyone that might wander too close. Several feet away from the tree, she stepped on something hard, knelt down, and found an ancient arrowhead. She rubbed her finger against the rough scores in the stone, and its sharp edge sliced into her finger.

"Ow!"

A drop of blood dripped onto the red sand. Kathleen gasped when she felt the sand beneath her feet shift; she was sinking. Trapped and unable to move, Kathleen struggled to get free when she heard a loud cracking sound coming from above her. She looked up and saw the twisted tree unravel itself before descending upon her. Its branches reminded her of arms loaded with spikes. She closed her eyes and screamed.

Kathleen opened her eyes and sighed. She was safe in her tent. The distant sound of a train whistle echoed in the night. She turned over and saw the dim glow from the dying fire through the walls of her tent.

Suddenly, she gasped.

The shadow of a lion travelled along the tent wall and stopped. Kathleen held her breath. The feline's majestic mane fluttered in the breeze. Gracefully, the lion sauntered away.

Kathleen rolled onto her back and exhaled.

Heart pounding, she lay with her eyes wide open, listening to the faint crackling sound of the dying fire. She grabbed her watch, pressed the little button on the side: a green light displayed the time—it was five minutes past three in the morning. Kathleen lay awake for the rest of the night, anxiously waiting for someone else to wake up.

CHAPTER 5

THE DIG

Femi pulled in front of the quaint little bistro, conveniently situated ten miles away from Kanzikuta Village and an hour away from Hanna's mobile laboratory, north of Tsavo National Park.

Safari, meaning *journey* in Swahili, was a hidden treasure nestled in the valley, surrounded by groves of acacia trees. Twice a week, tourists traveled by elephant with the aid of tour guides from Kanzikuta Village through the dry savannah and down the shallow gorge to the Safari restaurant. Only the locals knew its location by road.

He was early; he even had taken the time to stop at one of the clothing boutiques in Kanzikuta to buy a short-sleeved shirt to go with his tan-coloured pants.

Femi knew that it would take longer for Hanna to show up, especially if she got caught up in her investigation.

The sun dipped behind the trees.

He leaned back in his seat, took a deep breath, and exhaled slowly. He looked forward to having dinner with Hanna, but a wave of anxiety had managed to creep up on him. Why was it so important for Hanna to talk about feelings and about the past? Why dwell on such things? How he missed Sandra, her love, and the way she understood him. Femi shook his head. He pushed his thoughts away and tried to focus on the list of things he had to do the next day.

The sound of a car door slamming jolted him back to reality; he hadn't noticed the arrival of the black cube van that was now stopped behind him. He slid down in his seat and watched from his side view mirror as the door on the passenger side slid open. Two men wearing sunglasses, jeans, and black short-sleeved T-shirts jumped out and leaned against the vehicle.

All of a sudden, a man wearing a long, dark leather overcoat exited the restaurant. Femi was unable to read his face, for he also hid behind dark sunglasses. He strode over to the van and leapt inside, followed by two of the men, before sliding the door shut.

Femi looked away from the mirror when he saw the driver staring in his direction; it was almost as if he knew he was there. The man wasn't wearing any sunglasses.

They sped off; black smoke spewed from the exhaust as the tires skidded over the dirt, pelting stones and gravel.

That's odd! Why would they be in such a rush, and why were they all wearing sunglasses when it is virtually dark outside? he asked himself.

Suddenly a gentle tap on the jeep's door startled him; it was Hanna. Her radiant smile and sparkling eyes melted his heart. She wore a beautiful red, long wraparound skirt with a matching top.

He stepped out of the jeep and took her hands in his.

"You look beautiful," he said to her, kissing her lightly on the cheek.

"Thank you," she said, smiling.

As they stood looking at each other, Femi felt his anxiety returning. He looked into the night and thought of the men.

While holding her hand, he gently placed his other hand on the lower part of her back and guided her towards the road where the van had been minutes ago.

"Where are we going?" she asked.

Femi didn't answer. He squatted down and examined the tire tracks and the men's shoeprints. The dim light from the restaurant's front porch made it difficult to see, but he knew by looking at the tread marks that this vehicle was from the city.

"Femi, are you going to tell me what you're doing?"

"Sure, but first I want you to stand over here," he said, placing her in the exact spot where he had seen the driver. He then backed away toward his jeep to observe.

"Femi, I feel ridiculous," she said.

He knew by the change in the tone of her voice that she was getting upset.

He hurried back over to her. "I'm sorry, Hanna. I wanted to see if your eyes sparkled in this light."

"And did my eyes sparkle?" she asked. Her beautiful smile mesmerized him. Relieved, he smiled back.

"Absolutely." He gazed deep into her eyes and felt a sudden urge to kiss her. "Should we go inside?" he suggested, fighting the temptation. He truly liked her, but he didn't want to rush into something they both might regret later.

Once inside, they were escorted by a young, attractive black woman through a dark maze. They were surrounded by a sea of twinkling lights emitted from candles positioned around the room and from the centerpieces on each table. Trees were arched over doorways and positioned to create privacy for their guests.

The woman guided them to a table for two by a window. A waiter appeared and held out a chair for her to sit on before he gently pushed it in. He then proceeded to pour each of them a glass of white house wine before disappearing into the kitchen.

"Wow! This is beautiful! Have you eaten here before?" asked Hanna.

"No, I haven't, and so far I'm impressed."

The woman who had escorted them in returned to light a small candle and placed it in the center of their table before walking away.

The waiter reappeared, presented them with menus, and gave them a brief rundown of the day's specials before gracefully leaving them alone to decide.

"So?" she said, leaning forward. Her expressive brown eyes searched his.

"So . . ." said Femi, waiting for her to continue.

"Are you going to tell me the real reason why you made me stand in the middle of the road in the dark?" Hanna leaned back in her chair and crossed her arms.

"Oh! That!" he said.

The waiter reappeared. *Good timing,* he thought.

"Can you give us a few more minutes to decide, please?" she asked the waiter.

"Yes, miss," he answered.

Femi watched as his way out walked away. What should he tell her? He decided to tell her the truth.

"Well," she said, waiting impatiently as she drummed her fingers on her arm.

He leaned forward and whispered, "Just before you arrived, I saw two men waiting by a van. Another man exited the restaurant wearing a long leather overcoat. All of them were wearing sunglasses, except for the driver."

Hanna shrugged her shoulders, "So? Why are you telling me this?"

"So, the driver's eyes were red."

"Not only animals' eyes reflect light, you know that," she said before taking a sip of her wine.

"Yeah, I know, but this was different. The intensity in his eyes was bright; it was like I was looking at a nocturnal animal staring in the headlights, only he was human, and the lighting was next to nothing.

"I made you stand outside at exactly the same spot, under the same conditions, and your eyes didn't appear red at all. They were dark and twinkled. It was rather nice," he admitted. He took a sip of his wine; he was feeling nervous again. "Besides, why would they be wearing sunglasses in the dark?" he added.

The waiter returned. They placed their orders before Hanna excused herself, leaving him alone at the table.

She returned a few minutes later.

"Is everything all right?" he asked, noting her quick return.

"Yes, thank you." She paused and smiled at him before continuing. "I went to ask the bartender if he knew the man you were talking about," she explained.

Femi leaned forward, interested in what she had to say.

"He is a mortician from Nairobi, Dr. Mekufa. For over a decade, he has been the specialist who has taken upon himself to examine and report the cause of deaths in all these attacks."

"That's interesting!"

"What?"

"I was just speaking with Constable Whitmore this afternoon. I've asked him to fax me the reports on the lion attacks."

"Will he?"

"Reluctantly, but he said that he would," replied Femi.

Later in the evening, after paying the bill, they exited the restaurant. He walked her over to her car, kissed her on the cheek, and watched her drive away into the night.

Femi walked over to his vehicle and sat down. He was in a great mood. He liked her and believed that she felt the same about him. Dinner had gone well, and each had been so interested in what the other had to say that neither of them had noticed how late it was.

While driving toward Tsavo East National Park, Femi noticed the same van from earlier, parked on the side of the dirt road. He stopped the jeep, reached under the front passenger's seat, and grabbed his sturdy flashlight. He also grabbed his rifle from the backseat and loaded it before stepping outside.

A gentle, cool breeze rustled the tall grass. Femi shivered.

As he walked along the road toward the vehicle, the crickets ceased chirping in sequence for a moment before resuming their deafening chant after he had passed. He flashed his light at the ground to ensure that he was safe from snakes or other nocturnal creatures that might be lurking in the shadows. He approached the van and examined the tire tracks; this was no doubt the same van. He leaned his head against the glass to get a look inside; it was empty. Garbage littered the floor, dirt was smudged on the interior console, and the leather seats had been torn. Femi scanned the dashboard with his light. He tried the sliding door; it was unlocked. He opened it, peered inside, and frowned. On each seat, a pair of sunglasses had been placed on top of neatly folded clothes. He recognized the black leather overcoat the mortician had been wearing earlier. Their boots and shoes were placed on the floor in front of their seats.

He closed the door and directed his flashlight toward the surrounding darkness; no one was in sight. He checked for footprints, but there were none. *Where did they go?*

* * *

She opened her eyes to the sound of heavy breathing. She quickly got dressed and stepped outside her tent. She couldn't believe that she had fallen back to sleep, especially after what she had witnessed earlier in the morning. Now it felt like it had been a distant dream.

The tall teen who had been watching her yesterday was doing push-ups nearby.

"Good morning!" he greeted her.

"Hi! What are you doing?" she asked.

"Training."

"For what?"

He stopped to look at her. "The Olympics," he replied in a serious tone before stretching his legs. "I run every morning before it gets too hot. Lucas, one of the cooks, was kind enough to volunteer to help me. He will be keeping time and recording my progress."

"That's great! Have a good run!" she said before walking away.

"I don't believe we've been properly introduced," he called after her.

Kathleen turned around.

"My name is Sekani Kaita."

"Kathleen Gallant."

"I'd better go before Lucas changes his mind."

A black man wearing a white, long-sleeved culinary overcoat with long white pants waved at Sekani.

"Fine by me. Go and break your time!"

"Thanks," he said and ran over to Lucas.

Kathleen watched Lucas and Sekani walk over to a tree. Sekani got ready: with his hands on the ground, he dug his running shoes into the dry earth. She couldn't hear them, but Lucas must have said *"Go!"* because Sekani started to run away from the camp. The circuit seemed to be quite long, for he ran a great distance away before turning and making a perfect circuit back to the finish line.

Kathleen entered the dining area and was shown to her seat. Moments later, she was enjoying a hearty breakfast of bacon, scrambled eggs, toast, and a glass of orange juice. *How delicious! I didn't expect they'd have American cuisine,* she thought.

By the time she was finished, others had arrived, some eagerly waiting for the day to start, and others sauntering in half-asleep and grumpy.

After everyone had eaten, Professor Holdsworth and Michelle Standfort had everyone stand outside with their teams.

"Oh no! We were supposed to have decided on a name for the team, and a place to dig," said Okechuku.

Kathleen walked away from the crowd, toward the cliff, and stopped.

"What's up?" Okechuku had followed her.

Kathleen glanced at him and without saying a word continued toward the twisted tree, similar to the one from her dream. She carefully scraped the sand with her running shoes, lifting a few inches of red dust to reveal, like in her dream, an arrowhead. "That's strange," she whispered.

"All right! Team one! Do you have a name?" Professor Holdsworth called out to them. Kathleen saw the professor waiting impatiently. She looked at Okechuku and back to the professor before shouting back.

"Yeah! We have a name." Kathleen saw Kianga look at her with curiosity.

"We do?" said Okechuku, surprised.

"It's *Mchanga Ya Kale*, and we are going to dig right here."

The professor leaned over to speak with the coordinator.

Hands on her hips, Kathleen waited impatiently for the professor's response.

Kianga looked from Kathleen to the professor. She seemed to be anxiously waiting for a response too.

"All right, as you wish," agreed Professor Holdsworth.

Kianga stood up and threw her arms up in the air to show her disapproval.

"It's not even one of the sites, Kat," commented Okechuku. The site Kathleen had picked was several feet away from the designated, yellow-staked area.

"I know. I've got a hunch that something is under here."

"What does the name mean?" he asked.

"Beats me!"

"It means 'ancient sand,' idiots," retorted Kianga as she sauntered over. "How could you not know what it means? You're the one that picked it," she said, keeping her distance from them. "Anyhow, we shouldn't be digging near that tree."

"Why?" asked Okechuku.

"Never mind," replied Kianga. She spun on her heels and marched toward the group.

Kathleen and Okechuku looked at the tree. *Where did I hear of the name 'ancient sand' before?* she wondered.

The professor motioned for them to return to the group.

Soon the team names were established: team two, *Rafiki*, meaning *friend*, and team three, *Mvua*, meaning *rain*.

"Everyone did an excellent job choosing a name for zeir team," said Michelle, "and ze winner for ze best-picked name is . . . Mchanga Ya Kale Great job! Ze next assignment is to get to know your teammates."

A unanimous groan rose from the crowd of teens.

"I will give you a week to get to know your teammates. At ze end of ze week, you will be quizzed. Ze team who knows the most about each odder will win ze next prize.

All right! Before we get started wit' our excavation, Mchanga Ya Kale, please step forward to collect your prize."

Kathleen and Okechuku approached Mrs. Standfort, who was holding a box containing white baseball caps. The name Tsavo National Park was written on them in brown, and a picture of the sunset overlapped with the silhouettes of trees and a herd of elephants marching in the distance.

Kathleen grabbed one and handed it to Kianga.

Surprised, Kianga snatched her prize and looked away.

Kathleen donned her hat, grabbed a shovel, marched over to their site, and began digging into the hard soil. Okechuku followed her. Kianga reluctantly joined them, working as far away from the tree as possible.

After fifteen minutes, Kathleen's arms started to ache, and sweat rolled down her back. She stuck her shovel into the hard ground only to watch it fall over. She walked away, sat down under the tree, looked up at the thorny branches, and laughed at herself when she remembered her dream.

All of sudden the leaves rustled. Kathleen frowned, for the air was still, yet the leaves were swaying. And then she heard a low whisper. She crawled away on her hands and knees and turned to stare at the tree. The leaves had stopped moving.

Okechuku stopped digging and sat beside her. "I wonder if anyone else was having any luck."

She ignored him, her thoughts still lingering on the tree.

"Kathleen, what are you doing?" he asked.

"Nothing," she answered, getting up. She looked at the other teams and saw that one team was on break, while the members of another were down on their knees with their fine brushes, looking at something.

"Looks like they've found something," he observed.

"Hey, *Mzungu*! Throw me my water," ordered Kianga.

Kathleen reached for Kianga's water bottle, and threw it hard and high enough that it flew over Kianga's head and landed in the dirt a few feet away.

Kianga glared at her.

Kathleen gave her a sarcastic smile.

They walked over to the Mvua team, whose members were on all fours, lightly brushing dirt away from an object.

"Looks like you've found something," said Okechuku.

"Yeah, check it out!" said Tanisha. She moved aside so Okechuku and Kathleen could see. The shattered remains of a clay pot were slowly being uncovered with every stroke.

"Good work, *Mvua*," said Professor Holdsworth as he looked at their find. He looked up at the sky, removed his hat, and scratched his head. "Looks like rain, but I think we can work for a little longer. I have tarps in the back of the truck, so at the first sign of rain, cover your sites, and weigh the tarps down with rocks."

Half an hour later, fat raindrops began spattering the dry earth. Kathleen and Okechuku ran over with a tarp to cover their site while Kianga left them to fend for themselves, disappearing inside her shelter box.

Sekani rushed over to help them. By the time they were done, a torrential downpour pounded the ground. The three of them ran from the site to the shelter of the dining room. Large, clear plastic sheets covered the white drapery that surrounded the dining area.

On his way to sit down with his teammates, Sekani stopped to speak with Kathleen. "Kat, do you want to join us?"

"No, thank you!" she replied before sitting down beside Okechuku.

She watched Sekani walked away. He sat down beside Chase at another table across from her. He looked up at her. Their eyes held for a moment before his attention was stolen from her when Lisha and Adesina sat down beside him.

"You know, usually people take the opportunity to leave. You don't have to sit with me if you don't want to," said Okechuku.

Kathleen turned to look at him. "I'm sitting here because it's where I want to be."

Okechuku looked at her, surprised. "No one has ever said that to me."

"I trust you, Oke. You're a nice guy. Usually people want to chill with me, not because they like me or care—it's all about whose cool and who's not. They want me to hang out with them because I'm pretty . . . They're shallow and pathetic."

"Oh! Is there a slight possibility that we can be more than friends?"

"Not a chance," Kathleen responded. They both looked at each other before bursting into laughter.

Fifteen minutes later, the rain stopped. Kathleen and Okechuku walked outside. The hot sun dried the topsoil within minutes.

"Where's Kianga, anyway?"

"Probably in her tent," he replied.

Kathleen had stepped away from their campsite to have a look at a faint rainbow arching over the mountain when she noticed a dark shadow within the cliff, fifty feet over their site.

"What's up?" asked Okechuku.

"Huh? Oh! Nothing. Do you want to get started on our site?" she asked when she saw the other teams removing the tarps off their excavation sites.

"Sure! Should we tell Kianga?" asked Okechuku.

They walked over to her shelter, and Kathleen tapped on the wooden frame.

"Are you coming?"

"Get lost, *Mzungu!*" she shouted.

"Suit yourself," she replied before walking away with Okechuku.

"What's up with her? She acts like she doesn't want to be here," said Kathleen.

"She probably doesn't. I was speaking to Sekani, and apparently some of us were forced to join the camp. It was either that or wind up in some kind of trouble or homeless or in jail."

"You're kidding!"

"No."

"I thought this was their summer vacation."

"It is, but only for the month of August. It's not like back at home, where we have two months off. They go to school for three months at a time, and then they're off in August, December, and April."

"That's different."

"That's not all. In order to go to school, most have to travel away from home. They live in boarding schools and look forward to going home."

"And now they've been sent away from home, again."

"Precisely."

"Why?" she asked.

"Some parents have to work away from home, too, so they can't be there for their kids."

"That sucks."

"Yeah!"

"I wonder what Kianga's story is."

"I don't know."

They peeled away the tarp and started to dig again.

"Why did we have to cover the soil with a tarp? Wouldn't the rain have softened this rock we have to dig through?" asked Kathleen.

"Maybe it's to prevent flooding."

"You're probably right, Oke," she agreed.

After an hour, Kathleen sat down to drink some water. Her arms ached, and her skin had started to burn; she immediately applied more sunscreen.

Okechuku stretched his back and sauntered over to Kianga, who had finally joined them but was keeping her distance.

"Hey! What's up with the tree?" whispered Okechuku.

Kianga stopped to look at him, and when she saw he was serious, she sighed. Leaning over, she began whispering what she knew to him. "All right! Trees are channels to the dead."

"What do you mean?" asked Okechuku.

"I mean . . . it's a perfect medium for spirits to hang out."

"Don't believe everything you hear, Oke, especially from this one!" shouted Kathleen as she picked up her shovel.

Kianga ignored her comment and took a swig of her water.

The scraping sound of Kathleen's digging masked their conversation.

"Do you really believe that?" he continued.

"Yeah! Look at it!"

"Yeah, I'm looking, and I only see a tree."

"But I see a tree with two souls. Look at the two trunks, twisted together to form one. It's evil and probably keeping a good soul captive."

"Right! As if!" he said. "How can you tell that it's evil?" he asked, trying to make conversation.

"Look at it."

Okechuku looked at the tree. One of the trunks was thicker and healthier-looking than the other. The smooth bark seemed unscathed, except where the other tree had intercepted it, causing the bark to split where it had to compensate for space to grow.

"I don't believe in ghost stories," he said after examining the tree from a distance.

"Suit yourself, but I know for a fact that a tree like that one is evil. There once was this woman who went missing. Five years later, a group of boys were walking in the forest when they came across a twisted tree, like this one. They decided to cut it down." Kianga grabbed her shovel.

"What happened?"

"I don't know! All that they found were their axes, but that evening, the missing woman had returned."

"And the boys?"

". . . were never to be seen again."

"Did the woman say anything?"

"Nope. She won't talk . . . gone crazy. Some say the tree released her when the boys were captured."

"Impossible."

"Yeah? Then where's your girlfriend?"

Okechuku spun around. Kathleen was gone; her shovel was leaning against the tree.

CHAPTER 6

THE CAVE

While Okechuku and Kianga were whispering to each other, Kathleen took the opportunity to sneak away and scale Babu Mountain. She had been curious about the shadow she'd seen earlier and had always wanted to try mountain climbing, but the opportunity had never presented itself until now. At home, when she wasn't immersed in her studies, she had violin lessons to attend and tennis matches to play.

Halfway up the rock wall, Kathleen's forearms and fingers began to ache. Sweat beaded on her forehead, stinging her eyes. Instinctively, Kathleen wiped her forehead against her arm, knocking her hat off and smearing the oils from her face into her eyes. Her eyes began to water. The burning and itching became unbearable.

She glanced below, but she could no longer see past her tears; she couldn't tell where her hat had fallen or if anyone had seen her.

She blinked hard while continuing her ascent. She persevered, searching the flat rock with her tired and sweaty fingers for grooves and crevices.

The thought of falling didn't cross her mind until her foot slipped.

Finally she reached the ledge, and with a great effort, she pulled herself onto her stomach before lifting one leg over at a time. She sat down with her legs dangling over the edge of the cliff and immediately wiped her eyes with the bottom of her T-shirt.

Once she was able to see and the burning of her muscles had subsided, Kathleen glanced behind her and smiled. There was a cave.

Excited by her discovery, she reached into her front pocket to retrieve a tiny keychain-flashlight. She got up and cautiously made her way over to the cave. Sunlight bathed the rocky floor of a wide, low-ceilinged entrance. Entering was difficult, for large boulders lay scattered on the ground, making it nearly impossible to walk straight ahead without stubbing one's toes or bumping one's knees. Once she stepped into the darkness and away from the natural light, she switched her tiny light on—which didn't do much for illuminating her path. Within several feet, the floor sloped downward, and the ceiling disappeared. She descended carefully, sending a small avalanche of rocks skittering down the slope with a loud, exaggerated echo.

She squinted while waiting for her eyes to adjust. The air felt cool and wet on her skin, giving her the shivers, and the musty smell made her nose wrinkle. From the echoes of her footsteps, she sensed she had entered a large room—a cavern. She straightened and began searching blindly for a wall when she heard the sound of a small avalanche coming from farther inside the cave, reminding her of the dangers of spelunking. Kathleen stopped.

She spun around, shining her light—more for her sense of security than of sight.

"Hello! Is anyone there?" she called out, but the only sound she heard was the echo of her own voice. She resumed exploring when she heard more rocks fall, but this time the sound seemed closer.

Kathleen froze; the thought of a wild animal stalking her was unnerving.

An eerie silence fell upon her; something didn't feel right. She had to leave. Kathleen spun around and had started back toward the entrance when she tripped, dropping her keychain-flashlight. Had she been able to see, she would have noticed the large boulder positioned directly in front of her. As she fell forward, her head smacked against the rock before her hands could break her fall.

A sharp, acute pain shot from her forehead to the back of her head. She rolled to her side and tried to sit up, but a wave of dizziness pinned her down. She touched her forehead and winced, for it stung. Her fingers felt wet and sticky; she was bleeding.

Her heart raced when she heard the sound of footsteps approaching her. Frightened, she began crawling, pushing with her legs and clawing with her hands over the dirt and rocks, trying to drag herself away.

A loud ripping sound, like the tearing of cloth, resonated through the cave. Kathleen gasped when she felt the touch of a hand on her shoulder before it turned her over slowly.

She tried to sit up, but her head felt too heavy to lift.

"Don't move," said a male voice.

He held her head in his lap and brushed the hair away from her face before placing something soft on top of her wound. She winced in pain as he applied pressure to stop the bleeding.

"Who are—?" she tried to speak but the excruciating pain prevented her from doing so.

"Shhhhh!" The man stroked her hair before removing the cloth and reapplying it with more pressure. Even though she couldn't see her caregiver, a sense of calmness and of relief washed over her.

In the distance, Okechuku's voice boomed from outside the cave, followed by another voice she didn't immediately recognize.

He gently lifted her head before laying her down on the ground. He then took her hand and placed it over the cloth before standing up. As fast as he had come, he was gone.

"Wait!" she said, the vibration from her voice shooting a stabbing pain through her head.

Her eyes stung when she saw two circles of light bouncing around. The sound of people running and calling her name echoed in the cave and pounded inside her temple and forehead.

Stop shouting! she pleaded silently.

A wave of dizziness overcame her as she began to drift in and out of consciousness.

"Over here!" she heard Okechuku call out.

She felt herself being lifted, making the blood rush to her head and transforming the dull throb into a massive pounding migraine. Kathleen moaned. Out in the warm sun, she opened her eyelids slightly and caught a glimpse of who was carrying her; it was Sekani. She closed her eyes and rested her head against his warm chest.

She moaned again in pain when the professor shouted for Dr. Racine. Her eyes fluttered open long enough for her to see Professor Holdsworth looking at her. She closed her eyes, not only because the sunlight burned them, but also because of the sudden guilt and shame she felt; she didn't mean to have caused so much worry and panic. And the professor, the look in his eyes—all she wanted was to forget.

A warm hand touched her forehead. She saw the doctor examining her closely before her world faded into blackness.

Kathleen woke up inside the nursing station and immediately shielded her eyes from the brightness with her hand when she felt bandages on her forehead.

"Hey!" said a familiar voice.

Okechuku was sitting beside her.

Sekani was standing at the entrance, his arms crossed in front of his chest, a smug look on his face.

"Hey!" she replied hoarsely, trying to sit up. "Ow!" she reached for her forehead. A dull pain pulsed through her head.

"Well, now that you are ugly, I don't think I want to be seen with you anymore," Okechuku said before flashing a bright smile.

"Get out of here," she teased. "What are you guys doing here?"

"Uh! Duh! I'm your buddy. You broke the buddy rule, you know," said Okechuku.

"I'm sorry, Oke. How did you find me?" she asked.

Okechuku held up her hat. "Found it at the foot of the mountain... figured you'd be crazy enough to climb it."

"What were you doing exploring a cave in complete darkness?" asked Sekani.

"I had a light," she replied.

"This little thing," he said, dangling her keychain-flashlight for her to see.

Kathleen blushed.

Sekani tossed her the keychain, which landed on the bed.

She remembered someone holding her inside the cave.

"Who helped me?"

"We all did . . . I mean, Oke got there first," explained Sekani before Kathleen interrupted him.

"No, I mean before any of you got there."

"Sorry, Kat. There was no one else there. By the time we got to you, you were passing out."

"Oh!" She looked at her palms; they were scratched. She looked around her bed. "Hey! What happened to what I was holding?"

"Do you mean this piece of cloth?" said Okechuku as he grabbed a white, bloodstained piece of material from the garbage pail and held it by the tip of his fingers, as if it were contagious.

Kathleen reached out for it.

Okechuku shrugged and handed it to her.

She examined the small piece of cloth. It had ornate, embossed symbols tracing the edges.

"What do you think this means?" she asked.

"What?" said Okechuku.

She showed it to him.

"Nothing! It's a piece of clothing, like the ones you buy in a store, Kat." He looked at her with concern.

"Where did you find that?" asked Sekani. He looked at her, pensively.

"I found it in the cave before I tripped," she replied, not wanting to tell them about her encounter. She remembered a presence in the cave, but now her thoughts seemed distant, like they were fading.

The professor marched in. Sensing that a lecture was coming, Okechuku and Sekani left.

"Feeling better?" he asked.

"Yeah!"

"What were you doing in that cave?" he asked.

"Exploring," she answered, knowing very well where this was going.

"And didn't I make myself clear about the buddy system and its importance?"

"Yes, sir," said Kathleen, staring down at her feet. She couldn't stand looking at the professor; she felt bad for the trouble she had caused.

"Do you know how dangerous these parts of Kenya can be, not to mention the caves? Did it ever cross your mind that the cave may be a hyena den? Do you know the danger you placed some of our staff members in, not to mention your friends? You are lucky we found you when we did."

"I'm sorry, Professor."

"If you try another stunt like that, you will be dismissed and sent to your father. Do I make myself clear, young lady?"

"Yes, sir."

"Good! Well, the doctor says that you will be fine and that the swelling should go down in a couple of days."

A dark, tall man dressed in a white culinary uniform walked in holding a tray.

"Ah! Just in time. Here is your supper," said the professor.

"Supper?"

"Yes! You've slept all afternoon, and the doctor suggests that you stay here for the night. Tomorrow, we have a field trip. I'm sorry, but you won't be able to join us. You can take the time to recover while we're gone, so enjoy your food, Kathleen!" he added before leaving.

The next day, Kathleen was awoken by voices booming from outside.

Okechuku popped into her small recovery room; his brilliant smile and cheerful personality made her laugh. Kathleen winced in pain.

"What are you doing here?" she asked, touching the bandage on her forehead.

"Just checking to see if you're okay."

"Yeah! I'm fine . . . bored, but otherwise okay," she said.

"Yeah! I wish you were coming."

"Don't! I prefer staying back, anyway," she said while looking around at her surroundings. "You should go before they leave without you."

"Okay, see ya later! By the way, Sekani likes you," he added before leaving.

Kathleen smiled. She liked Sekani. He was very good-looking, but since her breakup with Shayne, she was reluctant to get involved with anyone. Kathleen had truly fallen for him and had thought he felt the same way about her. But his true feelings were revealed when a vicious rumour traveled through the school and found its way to her by mistake; apparently, Shayne had been seen kissing her best friend, Lucy. After she confronted him, he didn't deny or confirm the rumours; he had simply shrugged his shoulders, laughed at her, and walked away.

For two months, she cried herself to sleep. The pain was unbearable, crushing her will to leave the house. Humiliated and hurt, she avoided all contact with her peers. Where she thought there was friendship, she found betrayal; the guised empathy from her so-called friends fed the voracious appetites of gossipers. If she had known that love could be so hurtful, she would have never opened her heart. With the shattered pieces from her broken heart, she built a wall, guarding herself with distrust.

Later that year, Lucy came to her in the schoolyard, sobbing. She told her how Shayne had dumped her for another girl. Kathleen stared at her in disbelief before standing up and walking away.

Over the next few days, whenever their paths crossed, Lucy stared at her, her eyes brimming with tears, but Kathleen ignored her.

The drama soon escalated when Shayne stopped her and asked if she would go out with him on a date, within earshot of Lucy, who was having her lunch nearby.

Kathleen remembered looking up at him and had just enough time to say, "You've got to be kidding," when a distraught Lucy charged over. Blinded by rage, she stood in front of Kathleen.

"All right! Cat fight!" she recalled him shouting.

Kathleen, who was certain that Lucy was going to throw a punch, spun around and slugged Shayne in the jaw. It was then she learned the truth about how Shayne had manipulated her, and that Lucy had never intended to hurt her. Shayne walked away, humiliated to have been hit by a girl in front of his friends. Kathleen realized that her and Lucy had been through enough and started hanging out with her again.

The professor entered the tent, snapping Kathleen out of her flashback. He wished her well before leaving to join the others. As the bus drove away, Kathleen grabbed her backpack, which Okechuku had brought her the night before, and began to work on postcards to send to her mother and baby brother.

Half an hour later, the doctor arrived for her routine checkup: taking her blood pressure, checking her temperature, and examining her pupils to make sure she hadn't suffered a concussion. The doctor removed her bandages and applied a fresh dressage to her wound before rewrapping her head.

After breakfast, Kathleen decided to stretch her legs. She walked out to their site and grabbed a shovel.

Expecting the soil to be rock-hard, like the day before, Kathleen drove the shovel hard into the ground. To her surprise, the shovel sank into the earth with ease.

That's strange! Why is the soil easier to dig today? she thought with each shovelful. Whenever she dug a hole, the walls crumbled and collapsed. It made it easier for her, and before long, she had dug a good-sized rectangular hole.

A sudden tap on her shoulder startled her.

"Dr. Racine." She gasped.

"Sorry, Kathleen. I didn't mean to startle you." She handed her a bottle of water. "You should take it easy. You don't want to overexert yourself."

"I'm all right, Doctor. Do you mind if I work a little longer before I have lunch?" she asked before taking a drink of her water.

The doctor surveyed the hole she had dug with a puzzled look on her face.

"Looks like you've done quite well for yourself," she said.

Kathleen had a thought. "Doctor, after lunch, do you mind if I take a nap in my tent?" she asked, knowing that her question would give her the slack she'd been looking for.

"That sounds like a great idea, but don't work for too much longer."

"I won't," she agreed.

The doctor gave her a pat on the shoulder before heading back to the campsite.

After lunch, Kathleen retired to her tent, stuffed some of her clothing under her sleeping bag, grabbed her flashlight, stuck it into her backpack, and snuck out. She took a good look around. *Great! No one in sight!*

She stealthily scaled the escarpment while checking periodically over her shoulder to see if anyone had seen her. The bandages made a great sweatband, absorbing any excess moisture.

When Kathleen reached the cave's entrance, she took out her flashlight, flipped the switch on, and entered. Rocks were scattered throughout the entrance, making a pattern like a chessboard. *An avalanche must have occurred here sometime,* she thought. This time, the flashlight she'd taken with her illuminated the cave's floor adequately. "No wonder I fell."

She descended the steep slope of the tunnel, walking around boulders; it was a miracle she hadn't injured herself on her way in the first time. Once on level ground, she spotted something white gleaming in the distance. As she got closer, she noticed that it was a teenager, sitting with his knees slightly drawn up, his elbows resting on them, holding his head between his hands. Long dreadlocks cascaded over his shoulders and down his back.

"So, you've come back," he said, his deep voice reverberating through the cave. He glanced at her quickly before looking away. "Do you mind not flashing that light at me?"

"Sorry," she apologized before redirecting her light at the wall. He wore a long-sleeved white cotton tunic and long white pants that almost hid his dark bare feet.

"You really shouldn't be here," he said without looking at her.

"I wanted to thank you," replied Kathleen, keeping her distance.

"You really didn't have to," he said. He spoke English well, with only a slight African accent. "How are you feeling?" he added.

"All right," she said. She walked over to the wall beside him, turned around, and caught him glancing at her before looking at the floor between his feet.

"Why are you sitting here alone in the dark?"

"You're not from around here, are you?" he asked, ignoring her question.

Curiosity danced inside her, giving her a desire to know more about him. It was not like her to delve into someone else's business, but for some reason, she felt bold and intrigued.

"No, I'm not," she answered, trying to be elusive with her answers.

"You should leave," he repeated. "It's not safe for you here."

Kathleen glided her hands over the cave's wall, examining its smooth texture and ancient drawings while ignoring his warnings. She didn't feel frightened; instead, she felt a strange attraction toward him. She came upon a drawing of a woman with long hair holding a book high above her head. Straight lines were drawn from the book to the people surrounding the woman.

"Do you know what these drawings mean?" she asked, sneaking a glance at him before looking away, surprised by his lack of interest; usually boys were unable to keep their eyes off her.

"It's the story of what happened to my people."

"I'd like to hear it," she pried, wanting to hear his velvet voice.

"You must leave this country, Kathleen."

She turned to look at him, surprised that he knew her name. She had begun walking toward him when he held out his hand.

"Stop! Don't come any closer. You must pack your things and leave, *now*, before it's too late!"

Startled by the change in his tone, Kathleen backed away, confused, and wondered why, just moments ago, she had felt an unwavering desire to know him and to be with him. Now she was frightened and wanted to go back. She turned around and slammed her shins on a rock. *Why am I so clumsy?* she thought. She fell to the ground, clutching her legs. Her flashlight rolled a few feet away, shining its light on a nearby rock and then back onto her.

He immediately ran over to her and gently helped her up. She turned in his arms to face him before she gasped. His hair framed a gorgeous face, but his eyes . . .

She composed herself before nodding her head.

"Okay, I'll leave," she agreed, trying hard not to panic. She took a few steps, bent down to grab her flashlight and started to calmly walk away.

"Kathleen," he called after her.

His deep voice made her heart flutter once again. She didn't turn around to look at him; she stood silently, waiting for him to say something. She didn't want to leave, but was frightened by what she'd seen.

"I should go," she finally said.

"I can't leave the cave during the day," he explained. "The light hurts my eyes."

"What happened to your eyes?" she asked.

There was no reply.

She turned around to find him gone.

CHAPTER 7

THE VISION

She sauntered outside in a daze, not sure how to comprehend what she'd seen. At one glance his eyes seemed dark, opaque like expensive black pearls, but in another glance, depending on the light's angle of reflection, his eyes shone bright yellow. Kathleen stopped. She found a steep path leading down the mountainside to the campsite.

I was wondering how they'd managed to rescue me, she thought.

She clambered down the trail, occasionally glancing over at the site below, until she arrived behind the large tent. She peeked around the corner of the dining area and walked over to her tent to drop off her backpack and flashlight before heading over to her site.

She sat beside the hole she'd dug earlier, impressed with what she had accomplished. The other teens had barely scratched the surface, but Kathleen had dug a hole approximately two feet deep, two feet wide, and four feet long. She was determined to continue and prove to Okechuku and Kianga that she had made the right choice for a dig site.

All of a sudden her stomach felt queasy and a wave of dizziness washed over her. As she went to stand up, shooting pain cut through her head, pinning her down on the ground. She closed her eyes, holding her head between her hands while trying to cope with the pain. A series of bright pulsating light intensified her headache when the image of a torch burning in a distance flashed in her mind. She saw a dark tunnel and then a chamber. Inside were shelves laden with books, journals, and rolls of papyrus.

A shadow swept across the chamber. The light flickered.

"Kathleen, find it." A voice ordered her. She stepped closer towards a shelf at the far wall. "*Find it!*" it shouted at her. Another voice, speaking in another language, overpowered the other, becoming louder with every step she took, deafening her.

Before her, she saw a green leather book, gleaming in the dim light. Kathleen went to touch it, but quickly retrieved her hand when she saw rivulets of blood trickling from the book to the ground.

"Take the book!" the voice yelled. Immediately, she backed away. The voices stopped.

"Kathleen! Kathleen!" She heard her name. The visions of the chamber faded. Kathleen opened her eyes, looking bewildered, unable to comprehend where she was for a moment. Her intense migraine was gone, leaving her to cling to the nauseated feeling in her stomach.

"Get me some water," Dr. Racine ordered. Moses returned with a cup of water and handed it to the doctor. "Here, drink this."

Kathleen hadn't realized she was rocking until she went to reach for the water. The doctor put the glass down and grabbed her hands, making her stop. She then handed her the glass of water.

"Kathleen! Are you all right?" asked Dr. Racine.

Disoriented, Kathleen just stared at her. After a brief moment, she recognized the doctor. "What happened?"

"I don't know, but you were rocking back and forth, repeating something over and over in Swahili."

"Swahili? But I don't even know Swahili," said Kathleen.

The doctor helped Kathleen to her feet.

"Let's get you out of the sun."

Kathleen saw the cooks staring at her, and as they approached the nursing station, they scowled at her before disappearing inside their makeshift kitchen.

Moses remained and watched.

"What was I saying in Swahili?" she asked.

"I don't know," answered the doctor.

"She said, 'You shall not change the sands of time, for the one who beholds the night will never set you free' and then you kept repeatin' 'Leave or you'll die,'" Moses replied.

"Thank you, Moses," said Dr. Racine, guiding her in.

After Kathleen had slept for several hours and received Dr. Racine's approval, she exited the nursing station just in time to see the school bus pulling in.

Excited, she waited patiently to greet her friends.

"Feeling better, Kathleen?" asked the professor as he stepped out of the bus.

"Y-yeah! I—I do!" she stammered when she saw Moses staring at her, and when the professor walked away from her, he immediately headed over to him. She saw Lucas and the other cooks waiting nervously by the cooking tent.

This can't be good! she thought.

"Hey, Kat!" said Okechuku, stepping out into the sun.

"How was it?" she asked while keeping a watchful eye on the professor and Moses.

"It was awesome," he said excitedly. "You should have seen the Nasiche Wildlife Sanctuary. We also visited an orphanage for elephants; it was so cool! The baby elephants were so cute playing soccer with the caregivers."

Kathleen gave him a nervous smile; she was happy for Okechuku, but at the same time, she felt afraid of the effect her incident may have had on the cooks.

"I would have liked to have seen that," she finally said.

Sekani stepped off the bus and smiled at her.

Kathleen blushed; she remembered what Okechuku had said about him liking her.

She glanced over her shoulder and saw the professor walking towards her. Kathleen spun around and began walking over to her tent.

"Not so fast, young lady," said the professor before he guided her away from prying ears.

She looked past the professor and saw Sekani and Okechuku watching them.

"What happened here, Kathleen?"

"Uh! Nothing."

"I have the entire cooking staff wanting to quit on me. Why do you think?"

"How should I know?"

"Kathleen, these men have been frightened by something they have seen. I've managed to convince them to stay, but at a cost," he explained. "So what happened?"

"Kathleen!" called Dr. Racine. "Excuse me for interrupting, Professor."

The professor sighed with frustration before walking away.

"You have a call on the satellite phone. It's your father," she explained before handing her the phone.

"Great! Does he know?" she asked, covering the receiver with her hand.

"It's procedure to contact the parents when there has been an injury."

"It's just a bump on the head. Does my mother know, too?" she asked, annoyed and frustrated.

"Yes," she said before leaving.

Sekani and Okechuku watched her while Adesina, Lisha, Sadia, and Tanisha snickered.

Kathleen turned her back to them.

"Hi, Dad!"

"Kat, are you all right? The doctor said that you have injured your head."

"Yeah! It's nothing. I fell and have a small bump . . . nothing to be concerned about."

"Do you want to go home?"

"No, Dad. I'll be fine."

"Are you sure?"

"Yes. Don't worry. The doctor said that I'll be fine and to just take it easy."

"Okay, but if you want to go home at any time, just call. Okay?"

"Okay, Dad. I love you."

"I love you more."

Kathleen chuckled. "Bye, Dad!"

"I'll talk to you later, sweetheart."

She turned around and walked over to Okechuku.

"So how do I turn this off?" she asked.

Okechuku grabbed the phone and examined it for a quick moment before pressing a button.

"Are you okay? You look frazzled."

Kathleen looked at him and then at the cooking station. The cooks had returned to their work.

"I'm fine," she said. She didn't know what to tell him. She was confused. What had happened to her? Definitely she had a concussion or something, but how could she have spoken in Swahili? Could she have been repeating what the second voice had been shouting in her vision?

"I bet Blondie doesn't last another day here," said Tanisha.

"Oh, shut up!" said Kathleen. She saw Kianga smile.

In the dining area, Kathleen, Okechuku, and Sekani waited patiently for their food while everyone else was being served.

Eventually Moses marched over to them, dropped their plates of food on the table, and left, but not before glaring at Kathleen.

"What's up with him?" asked Okechuku.

Sekani turned to face Kathleen. "Kat, what's going on?" asked Sekani.

"Why do you ask?" she asked before taking a mouthful of potatoes.

"Why do you think?"

Kathleen looked at him innocently and shrugged her shoulders.

Kianga stretched across the table and leaned over to Kathleen. "Sorry, Buttercup, but batting your eyes like nothing happened is not always going to bail you out."

"Stay out of this," said Okechuku.

"Why don't you stuff yourself?" she snarled. "Oh. Too late."

"Watch your tongue," warned Sekani.

"And what are you going to do if I don't?" she taunted him, staring him down.

"Nothing. I was just wondering what makes a pretty girl like yourself to be always on the defence."

Kianga was about to say something but stammered.

"What do you know?" she huffed before getting up and walking away.

"What was that all about, Sekani?" asked Okechuku.

"I think there is more to her than meets the eye," he replied.

"Why do you care?" she asked, relieved that the conversation was taking another turn.

"Because I know for a fact that Kianga's hiding a secret," he explained.

"And?" he asked.

"And in time we will find out what it is," he concluded.

Later, Kathleen, Okechuku, and Sekani exited the dining area.

In the distance, they saw a vehicle approaching, a cloud of dust swirling behind it. Sekani recognized his father's jeep and went to greet him.

Femi stepped out and gave him a one-arm hug. "How are things?"

"Good! We went on a field trip, today, to the Nasiche Wildlife Sanctuary," he explained.

"Ah! How's Vanessa?" asked Femi.

"She's great, but she wonders when we will visit her again. I think she misses us."

"Yeah! Yeah!"

"So, what are you doing here? I wasn't expecting you until next week," asked Sekani.

"Is your professor around? I need to have a word with him," Femi said, surveying the savannah and their site.

"Okay, what's up, Father? It's not like you to just drop by, unless it was urgent."

"Have there been any lion sightings in the area?" he asked, ignoring his son's question. He took off his hat and wiped his forehead with the handkerchief he carried in his back pocket.

"No, not at all."

Kathleen, who was standing nearby, listened intently. *Why does he seem so concerned? Should I tell him about seeing a lion's shadow on my first night?* she wondered.

Sekani left, leaving Kathleen and Okechuku standing in front of Femi. Feeling completely out of place and not wanting to appear rude, Kathleen introduced Okechuku and herself.

"Hi, how do you like it here?" he asked, glancing at Kathleen's forehead and frowning.

"It's great!" said Okechuku.

Kathleen nodded.

At that moment, Sekani returned with the professor.

Femi and Professor Holdsworth walked over to the other side of the professor's truck to speak in private.

"Darn!" said Kathleen.

"Are you trying to eavesdrop?" asked Okechuku.

Kathleen smiled.

He grabbed her hand and led her over to the professor's truck while Sekani watched them, seemingly amused.

"Get down!"

She knelt down and smiled. *Finally, someone who thinks like me!* she thought.

They crawled under the vehicle. Okechuku had a little more difficulty squeezing under it than Kathleen. She saw the professor's running shoes and the ranger's work boots.

"No, I haven't seen any lions—or any other creatures, for that matter. It's been fairly quiet," she heard the professor reply.

"I've heard back from Dr. Blackwell," announced Femi.

"I was wondering if we were going to hear from her again. I haven't run the camp without her before, and I've been fortunate not to have found any items needing examination by an anthropologist yet."

"Well, that brings me to my next question. Dr. Blackwell wanted to know if any of the students have come across any artefacts that might date back to the time of the Mchanga-Misitu War."

Kathleen looked at Okechuku, frowning. Okechuku shrugged.

"No, so far we have found an old vase and a couple of spearheads, but all of them seem to date to more recent times. Do you know why she's asking?"

"Not really . . . she believes to have found a correlation, as she puts it, between the attacks and the finding of ancient artefacts from the Mchanga-Misitu era."

"Attacks? I don't understand."

"She claims that everyone who has uncovered artefacts dated from that era has died."

"Died?" said the professor.

"Or, to be more exact, been killed," confirmed Femi.

"Killed? Why would someone kill another for an artefact? Are they that valuable?"

"The artefacts are not valuable, and they weren't killed by people."

"By what?"

"Lions."

"That's crazy. You can't possibly believe that lions are behind all of these killings. How many has it been?"

"She didn't say, but it has been going on for centuries. However, she said that this year, the killings have become more frequent."

"What should we do? Should we pack up?"

"No, not just yet . . . This doesn't add up."

"If Dr. Blackwell believes that lions are behind this, I believe her."

"I don't want to discredit Dr. Blackwell, but I think there is more to these attacks. Let's not be too hasty. Nothing is conclusive. For all we know, this could just be a coincidence. All I ask is to keep a vigilant watch over your site. If anything turns up, give me a shout. Here's my number. If you can't get a hold of me, leave a message with the dispatcher," he said.

"All right!" said the professor before they walked back to the ranger's jeep.

Kathleen and Okechuku started to squirm out from underneath the truck. She heard the ranger's jeep engine rev before taking off. They had just gotten their heads cleared from under the jeep when

Kathleen saw the professor's shoes beside her. She straightened herself, brushed the dust off her clothing and helped Okechuku up to his feet.

"Wow! What do you think they—" he began before Kathleen elbowed him in the gut and flashed her eyes toward the professor, who was now standing behind him. Okechuku slowly turned around and looked up at him, pretending to look surprised.

"Oh! Hi there, Professor! I was just looking for my . . ." He turned to look at her. She smiled and gave him her cell phone.

"I found it," she said, unconvincingly. She knew the professor wouldn't fall for such a lame story. Besides, they were teens—who would believe them, anyway?

"How much did you hear?" asked the professor.

"We didn't . . ." he stopped when Kathleen cleared her throat. He looked at her with his big brown eyes.

"Not enough!" she said, crossing her arms in front of her chest. Okechuku followed her action. Out of the corner of her eye, she could see Sekani and Kianga watching them from a distance. "I think we have a right to know what's going on."

"Well, I'll let everyone know as soon as there is something to know," he said before turning away from her.

"What about the deaths?" she demanded.

Kianga was now looking at her intently.

"I don't know any of the specifics," he concluded before starting off toward the dig site.

"Professor?" she called out.

"Yes, Kathleen?" he replied, turning around in exasperation.

"How would you know if an artefact dates back to the Mchanga-Misitu War?"

"By its composition. The materials they used back then were different from other periods. For instance, the Misitu loved to use colourful minerals, such as lazurite. It's bright blue and was used on the tombs of the pharaohs, in Egypt. I can only assume that the Misitu traded with the Egyptians."

"Lazurite?"

"Yes, some artefacts have traces of the mineral, but the best way to confirm if it is lazurite is by having it analyzed in a lab. Will that be all, Miss Gallant?"

"Yes, Professor. Thank you."

Kathleen turned around and saw Sekani and Kianga looking at her.

Kianga immediately turned away and pretended to be preoccupied with something else.

"Hey! Has anyone seen my watch?" shouted Chase from his tent. "I swear I placed it beside my sleeping bag last night.

"No," said Kianga before shrugging her shoulders and entering her shelter box.

"I haven't seen it," said Okechuku.

A few team members who had overheard them talking sauntered over.

"Hey, Sekani, didn't you say that you couldn't find your chain with the gold cross a few days ago?" asked Joseph.

"Yeah, I still haven't found it."

"My bracelet is missing, too," said Amber.

Sekani glanced around before looking back at Chase. "Well, it's obvious, then," he said. Kathleen looked at the other girls, who were now standing around him, completely entranced by his every word.

"What?" asked Chase.

"We have a thief," he answered before stepping out of the circle. Chase, Amber, and some of the others grouped together. What began as a conversation soon changed into a heated shouting match, with accusations being fired in all directions.

Lost in her thoughts, Kathleen didn't notice that her friend had entered the circle of angry teens before he was shoved hard on the ground by Joseph.

"Get lost, *Mzungu!*" someone shouted.

She didn't know what came over her, but Kathleen rushed over to Okechuku's defence, jumping on Joseph's back. He flipped her over, grabbed her by her T-shirt, and was about to punch her in the face when from behind someone grabbed his fist in a tight hold, squeezing it until Joseph's face contorted in agony. Kathleen looked up and saw that it was Sekani, towering over both of them.

"If I ever see you hit a girl, or someone that is smaller than you, you're going to have to deal with me. And that goes for anyone," he said, making Joseph writhe in pain before releasing his hold.

The boy immediately clutched his hand, massaging it.

"I wasn't going to hit her," said Joseph.

Sekani glared at him.

Lisha, Adesina, Sadia, and Tanisha sighed in admiration.

Joseph nudged his sister before glaring at her. With her hands on her hips, Lisha huffed aloud, "Oh, grow up! You got what you deserve." She spun around on her heels and left, followed by Sadia, Adesina, and Tanisha.

Kathleen got up and straightened her T-shirt. She turned to go find Okechuku when she almost walked into Sekani's hard, muscular body. She looked up and smiled. He gave her a charming smile that made her heart skip a beat.

"Are you all right?" he asked.

"Yeah."

"You're very brave. I admire someone who puts their friends before themselves," he said.

"Uh, thanks," she said, embarrassed. "I'd better see if he's all right," she added, slipping away, feeling flushed.

"Sure, Kat!" he said, making her blush even more. She turned around to find Sekani's admirers glowering at her.

Kathleen and Okechuku walked over to their dig site.

Kianga stood where she was, overlooking the hole before she turned around to face Kathleen.

"Nice! Digging our own grave, are we? Very suiting!" she said sarcastically before marching past them, shoving Okechuku. "Watch it, *Mzungu.*"

"She's really getting on my nerves," said Kathleen.

"Why is everyone calling me *Mzungu*? I'm black, aren't I?"

"Of course you are, just a lighter shade," she said, smiling.

"Thanks for what you did back there," said Okechuku

"No worries. You would have done the same for me."

CHAPTER 8

THE CAUSE OF DEATH

Kathleen sat at the edge of her excavation site while Okechuku went to get some water.

Oh, no! Not again, she thought.

A wave of nausea washed over her, followed by a migraine. Kathleen leaned over and waited for the inevitable. The images returned, but now she saw a different library. Swirls of dust danced in the sunlight as it streamed in through the dirt-covered windows. A silhouette dashed across the aisle ahead of her. Kathleen stopped.

"Njeri," said a voice from behind the bookshelves. She leaned forward, peering between the books. She heard it again, but this time the voice came from behind her. Kathleen spun around and gasped.

A black woman stood in front of her, staring at her.

Kathleen backed away, turned around, and ran to the end of the aisle. Sunlight filtered through a window where an ornament of an antelope with long horns and black markings on its face and along its underside stood on the windowsill. She was cornered. Kathleen faced the woman and cowered to the floor.

The woman towered over her and called her Njeri.

Kathleen closed her eyes. Silence returned. She felt the hot sun bearing down on her. She opened her eyes. The woman was gone; the vision had ended.

Disoriented, she jumped into the hole and fell onto her hands and knees. A cool sensation washed over her; Kathleen shuddered.

"Great job on the digging, Kat!" Okechuku had returned.

Confused, she stumbled forward and grabbed her shovel. An unbearable sadness ripped through her. She fought tears, took a deep breath, and looked around.

"Kathleen, are you all right?" asked Okechuku.

Her eyes were open, but she saw nothing. The pain, the emptiness she felt inside, crushed her. She heard a voice and saw a plump boy standing on the edge of a hole, looking down at her. *Why was he calling me Kathleen?* she wondered.

"Hey, Kat! Snap out of it!" he shouted, jumping into the hole and splashing water on her face.

Kathleen shook her head and looked blankly at Okechuku.

"Kat," he said softly, looking deep into her eyes.

"Why are you looking at me like that?"

"Because a minute ago you were staring at me as if you didn't know who I was . . . and I just splashed water on your face . . . and you didn't react."

"Really?" Kathleen sat down. *What is wrong with me?* she thought.

"Do you want me to get you something?" he asked, concerned.

"No, I'm fine, Oke. Are you going to help me?" she asked, handing him a shovel.

Okechuku reluctantly took the shovel from her.

"Do you think we should dig somewhere else?" asked Okechuku.

"No! Why would you ask that? Did Kianga put you up to this? You don't have to help me if you don't want to. If you rather join the others, by all means do so. I'm staying here."

"Is that what you want?"

"Yes," Kathleen snapped. "I don't need your help."

Okechuku threw his shovel down and started to walk away, a hurt look on his face.

"Oke . . . I'm sorry. I don't want you to leave. Come and dig this hole with me. I need your help. I don't know why I said those things. I don't know what's happening to me," she explained, falling on her knees.

"Maybe you should speak to the doctor," suggested Okechuku.

"No!" she shouted, "I mean . . . I'll be fine, Oke. It's just . . ." she stammered before looking up at him and smiling.

"I don't know, Oke. Please stay. You're my only friend."

They waited in silence for a moment before he caved, grabbing the shovel. He immediately began working.

Kathleen watched him. *How can I tell him what is happening to me when I don't even know myself? One moment I'm fine, and the next I feel anger or sadness for reasons I don't understand.*

"Can I get everyone's attention?" shouted Professor Holdsworth, who was kneeling beside a large white linen cloth spread on the ground.

The teams reluctantly dragged themselves away from their work and gathered around him.

"I have placed the artefacts you've found here," he explained. "The prehistoric people used flint to build arrowheads, daggers, and axes. The reason they used this material is because of its ability to split in any directions, creating sharp edges," he explained.

The group crouched around the professor and began examining their findings.

"Professor, what was this one used for?" asked Adesina, who was kneeling in the dirt and had picked up one of the artefacts.

"It was used for skinning. See how wide and round the sharp edges were? With a quick motion of the wrist, you can skin an animal quite effectively."

"Gross," muttered Amber.

"Professor, how come the arrowhead I found doesn't resemble any of these?" asked Kathleen.

She saw Okechuku frown at her. Kianga leaned forward on her hands and knees and stared at her.

She pulled out the arrowhead she had found on her second day from her pocket and handed it over to the professor, who immediately began examining it with great interest.

"Where did you find this?" he asked, intrigued.

"I found it where we are digging," she admitted.

"Nice! Keeping your findings to yourself, are we?" snapped Kianga, sitting back on her feet.

Kathleen ignored her.

"This arrowhead, as you call it, is actually a flint dagger, and a very rare one. See how much care was used to create it?" explained the professor.

"Looks the same to me," commented Joseph.

"This dagger would have been used by someone of great importance," continued Professor Holdsworth before handing it back to her.

"This is *boring*. I'm hungry. Can we go and eat?" asked Chase, who had been standing behind the group, uninterested.

"Sure." The professor sighed. He began collecting the artefacts and placing them in the box. The group got up while Sekani and Okechuku stayed behind to help the professor.

"Kathleen, do you mind if I ask what made you decide to dig there?" asked Professor Holdsworth.

Kathleen was standing and dusting off her shorts when she replied, "I don't know. I thought it would be a great spot by the tree, and when I found the dagger, it only made sense to dig there," she lied. She didn't want to tell anyone about the dream she'd had.

"The dagger was lying on top of the sand?" asked the professor. A look of concern flashed in his eyes.

"Yeah . . . sort of . . . maybe a few inches below, but it was easy to find."

"On second thought, do you mind if I have another look?" he asked.

Kathleen shrugged her shoulders, reached into her pocket and was about to surrender it over to the professor when she saw traces of blue embedded into minuscule grooves in the stone. *Could this be lazurite? Could this dagger be one of the artefacts Dr. Blackwell was referring to?* she thought, feeling the blood drain from her face.

She quickly glanced at the professor and handed it over to him. To her surprise, the professor quickly shoved it inside his pocket and said, "Do you mind if I keep this? It's an interesting specimen."

"Sure," she said suspiciously.

"I couldn't help but notice your excavation site. You've made quite a progress; however, I wouldn't want you to be disappointed. I wanted to let you know, if you feel like moving to another site, you are welcome to do so," the professor added.

"No worries, Professor. She will not be disappointed," Kathleen replied with a bright smile before she walked away.

"Sekani, Okechuku!" called out the professor.

The boys turned around.

"How long has she been behaving like this?" asked the professor.

Sekani shrugged his shoulders. "Like what?"

"She seems very determined on pursuing her excavation in that particular spot, while others would have surrendered and moved on to another site by now. Another thing, she just referred to herself in the third person—like she was speaking about someone else. Do you know what she could have meant?"

"No," answered Sekani.

After a pause, Okechuku said, "She has been having a lot of migraines, Professor."

"Keep an eye on your friend, and if her headaches persist, let me know. Anyhow, you should go and have some dinner," he suggested before carrying the box away to his truck.

Sekani and Okechuku entered the dining area. Kathleen waved at them and smiled.

Sekani stopped Okechuku. "So what was that all about? Why was the professor asking about Kathleen?"

"I don't know, but something is definitely going on with her. When I first met her, she was fun, cheerful . . . but now, she seems different."

"How so?" asked Sekani.

"She practically bit my head off when I suggested that we move excavation site. Come, let's go before she gets mad at us for standing here."

Okechuku and Sekani sat across from Kathleen.

Kathleen pushed her plate away.

"Aren't you hungry?" asked Sekani.

"Lost my appetite."

"Don't you think it's odd, Kat, that you found a prehistoric dagger lying on the ground exactly where you decided to dig?" Sekani asked.

"No," she said. The knots in her stomach tightened. "So what? I found a dagger. Do you think someone deliberately put it there for me to find?" she continued. She looked at Sekani and at Okechuku, who raised their eyebrows at her.

"That's ridiculous. Why would someone do that?" she continued.

"You heard what Sekani's dad said," reminded Okechuku.

"Maybe these artefacts are deliberately placed in the open for others to find," said Sekani.

"So now I'm next," replied Kathleen. "How did we get from talking about my flint dagger to the Misitu artefacts?" she asked.

"We didn't say anything about the Misitu artefacts. His dad mentioned artefacts that belong to the Mchanga-Misitu era. Besides, we saw your reaction when you handed the dagger over to the professor," said Okechuku.

Kathleen got up.

"Where are you going?" asked Sekani.

"Out. I'm not hungry," she snapped and exited.

The next day, she watched Sekani perform his stretching routine while he waited for Lucas to finish helping the crew with breakfast.

"Interesting necklace," she remarked.

"Do you like it?" he asked, stopping his stretching long enough to look at her.

"If you're into that kind of thing. Does it symbolize anything?"

"Apparently it's supposed to ward off evil spirits. Senior Elder Gatimu from the Moja tribe gave it to me . . . you know, to keep me safe from the lions."

"Or lionesses," she added, smiling at him.

Sekani smirked.

"Well, it looks like Lucas is ready. I'll see you later, and try to stay out of trouble while I'm gone!" he emphasized.

Kathleen stuck her tongue out at him. She watched him join Lucas and waited; she was certain that he would turn to look back at her, and sure enough, he did. She smiled and waved at him. He returned the wave and watched her for a moment before continuing on his way. He stretched his arms and his legs and started digging his shoes into the ground before Lucas gave him the okay to start.

She quickly got up and grabbed her flashlight from inside her tent before running past the campsite and up the path leading to the cave's entrance.

Inside the cave, Kathleen kept her light low to the ground to avoid blinding him.

"You don't take warnings very well," his low voice echoed.

She glanced up and saw him standing, his back to her.

"Why did you ask me to leave?" she asked.

"Does it matter?"

"It does to me," she said.

"What if I told you that your life depended on it?"

"How can it? What's so dangerous about spending part of my summer digging in the dirt?" she asked incredulously. She hoped that he'd confirm what she'd overheard Sekani's dad say to Professor Holdsworth, or perhaps divulge the real reason for the deaths.

"Just take my word for it."

"I'm not taking anyone's word, especially from someone I've just met. I'm not leaving until I get some answers. Are you responsible for the deaths?"

He glanced at her and frowned before looking away.

"So you've heard of the deaths, and here you are, standing before me, unafraid."

"Should I be?"

"I'm not going to hurt you, if that's what you're thinking, but something else might."

"Why don't you look at me?" she asked, changing the subject.

He turned around, walked over to her, and gazed deeply into her eyes. Butterflies fluttered wildly inside her, creating feelings in her she had never experienced before.

"Don't I frighten you?" he asked, towering over her.

"No," she said, entranced. "Do you see well in the dark?"

"Yes."

"What's your name?" she asked.

He brushed a loose strand of her hair away from her face, taking her breath away.

"Sunjata."

"That's a beautiful name."

"How's your head?" he asked, his eyes drifting to her forehead.

"Fine. I can't wait to take these bandages off," she admitted.

"Here!" He gently unravelled her bandages from her head before gently stroking her face.

The butterflies returned, making her insides scream with excitement.

"All better now." He examined her head carefully, his warm hand gently turning her face to the left and then to the right. He softly stroked her hair and then backed away.

"I must go," he said before gracefully disappearing into the darkness.

The temptation to follow him was strong, but her fear of being caught and sent home was even stronger. She left the cave and hid her flashlight behind a rock. She then looked for a tree, broke off a branch, and brought it back, placing it over the flashlight to hide it.

During the day, Kathleen had difficulty keeping her excitement to herself.

"What's got into you today?" asked Okechuku.

"What? Can't a girl be happy?" She looked at him with large puppy eyes.

He raised his eyebrow at her with suspicion.

"All right, if you must know," she whispered. She beckoned him to come closer. *Should I tell him about Sunjata? I trust him, but I don't want to put him in an awkward position if he feels the need to tell someone,* she thought.

"We are about to embark on something big, bigger than your wildest dreams," she said, pulling herself away and smiling.

"What do you and Kianga take me for, a fool?" he scolded.

"I'm glad I'm not the only one who sees the truth," interjected Kianga, who was sitting nearby.

"Ignore her," Kathleen said dismissively. "I mean what I say. I don't exactly know what it is, but I know it will happen soon."

"And how do you know this?" he asked.

"Just call it girl's intuition," she said smugly before jumping to her feet and walking outside.

Later that night, Kathleen tossed and turned, thinking about her newfound friend. She couldn't wait to see him tomorrow. She set the alarm on her watch for 6:45 a.m., just before sunrise.

* * *

Dr. Mekufa examined the body of an African male in his late forties. The body had been found close to a water hole in the southwestern region of Kenya.

Shutters closed, blinds drawn, he worked in secrecy in the darkness of the morgue; the flickering light of a candle cast shadows along the walls of his office.

As he bent over the body, Dr. Mekufa noted lacerations on the chest and hands, four broken ribs, a punctured lung, and crushed metacarpals. He'd seen these types of injuries before; it happened more frequently than some liked to believe. Many locals, and especially tourists, thought that these animals were harmless, but it is quite the contrary. They were very territorial, and if provoked, they would attack. *Yes, this man definitely died from being attacked by a hippopotamus.*

He removed his latex gloves, walked over to his office, and recorded the date, the time, the victim's information, and the details of his examination. Dr. Mekufa paused for a moment before writing that the cause of the man's death was a lion attack. He then proceeded to fax the information to the constable's office.

Two men entered the room.

"You may cremate the body. I have completed the examination," said Dr. Mekufa. The men zipped up the body bag and carried it out of the room.

CHAPTER 9

HE LIKES ME,
HE LIKES ME NOT

In the early morning, Kathleen awoke up to the sound of her alarm beeping. She quickly donned her shorts, T-shirt, socks, and shoes and then quietly unzipped her tent. She stealthily snuck out and walked slowly around the tents to the path that led to the cave.

At the mouth of the cave, she saw the rays of the morning sun touch the mountainside, basking it in red. She grabbed the flashlight she'd hidden the day before from behind the rock and entered. Halfway down the slope, Kathleen stopped. Sunjata was standing a few feet away from her, shirtless, his muscular back to her.

Standing in front of him was a young man who nodded in her direction when he saw her.

Sunjata spun around. An angry growl escaped his pursed lips. Kathleen noticed that his jaws were clenched tightly, as were his hands.

"Sun . . ." a woman's sultry voice trailed off when she noticed Kathleen. She had appeared from deep inside the cave and stood several feet away from the man.

Sunjata turned back around to face them.

"Well, well, well, what do we have here, Sun?" asked an attractive, dark woman. A wry smile stretched across her face as she gracefully sauntered over, as if walking on a catwalk.

"Kathleen, this is my sister, Sade, and my brother, Eli," said Sunjata, without giving her so much as a glance.

Kathleen remained frozen; she felt uncertain and intimidated by them.

"I don't think I've ever met anyone as white as this little thang," said Sade, crossing her arms.

"*That's enough!*" shouted Sunjata, startling Kathleen.

"Whatever, Sun! Have your little fun," she said, shrugging her shoulders before taking another good look at Kathleen. She elegantly whipped her hair and body around before striding away. Her eyes glimmered yellow as she took one final glance at Kathleen before disappearing into the darkness.

"You probably told her," whispered Eli. His bright yellow eyes mesmerized her.

"No," muttered Sunjata.

"So, does Grandfather know about this?" he asked, glancing over to her and flashing a toothsome smile.

"Leave . . . *now!*" ordered Sunjata.

"All right! All right! I'm leaving. Take it easy! He will want to know," he said before following the same path as Sade.

Sunjata turned and glared at a confused Kathleen.

"Tell me what?" she asked. "What will he want to know?"

"Didn't I make myself clear? Don't come here anymore, and leave this country." Sunjata's voice quivered with anger.

Kathleen felt a lump growing in her throat and tears welling up in her eyes.

"I saw your little excavation. Which one is yours? Wait, let me guess . . . the one that looks like a grave."

Kathleen's bottom lip quivered.

"It wouldn't matter if I told you to stop. No . . . you just don't listen, anyway."

She stood before him, paralyzed with sadness, tears streaming down her face.

"Get out of here and don't ever come back!"

She dropped the sunglasses she had brought for him and ran from the cave. Blinded by tears, she ran down the path to her campsite and slammed right into Sekani.

"What are you . . ." he stopped when he noticed her sobbing. "What's wrong, Kat?" he asked, deeply concerned. He hunched over to look into her eyes.

"Nothing," she muttered before slipping away from his arms and disappearing inside her tent. She immediately zipped her tent closed, dropped down on her sleeping bag, and cried.

Sekani glanced up at the mountain. He noticed that she had been carrying a flashlight. He walked behind the site toward a small grove of trees.

"Sekani? Are you going to run today?" asked Lucas, ready to time him for his morning run.

"Not today, Lucas. I'm going to do some tracking," he explained.

"Just like your father," he replied before heading back inside the large tent.

Sekani grabbed his flashlight and followed her tracks up the mountain until he reached the cave's entrance, where her shoeprints ended. He entered, flashing his light on the ground and then on the walls. He glided his hand along the smooth wall, tracing over the prehistoric paintings before stepping back; it was then he saw the footprint of a man in the dirt beside a small heap of Kathleen's bandages.

Who could this be? It couldn't be someone from the camp, for we all wear shoes, he thought. He returned to the site where he decided to keep a closer eye on Kathleen.

Sweat beaded on her forehead as she continued to excavate while evading Sekani's stare. *Why is he always watching me? He must suspect something.*

She lifted her shovel of dirt and dumped it over the wall. The soil crumbled, caving in and refilling the hole she had just dug, giving way in some locations, while remaining rock-hard around the perimeter. She had guessed that the soil had been dug before, but her theory seemed flawed since, prior to their excavation, the ground was nearly impenetrable.

Her second theory, more unlikely than the first, was that someone wanted her to find something.

Okechuku worked quietly beside her, occasionally glancing in her direction. He asked her several times if she was upset with him, but the only response she'd given him was a shake of her head.

She was too choked up to speak, or to look at him; she'd feared that if she did, she might start crying. She loved how he respected her, never leaving her side, and not pressuring her with questions; she had definitely found a true friend.

He handed her a water bottle, which she immediately accepted while muttering a barely audible thank you.

They worked in silence until the red sun had abandoned them, dipping behind the horizon and casting the friends into darkness. Unable to see inside the hole anymore, they continued blindly until Kathleen's shovel hit a rock. At the same moment, three feet away, Okechuku's shovel crashed with an audible thud.

"What was that?" he asked.

"I don't know," she answered.

"Hey, Kathleen and Okechuku! Are you guys going to dig all night?" asked the professor, holding a lantern in his hand. Others had joined him, holding lanterns above their heads so they could see into the hole.

"Professor! I think we found something," said Okechuku.

The professor handed the lantern to Okechuku, grabbed the shovel that Kianga had thrown down earlier in her frustration, and jumped in.

As soon as his shovel hit the ground, it collided with something hard, sending vibrations up his arms. He dropped down to his hands and knees and began brushing dirt away. Okechuku handed the lantern to Kathleen and started helping. Soon, both of them had uncovered what looked like a grave. A pile of neatly stacked rocks, in shape of a pyramid, six feet in length by three feet in height, rested six feet under the now cold ground.

Everyone gathered around the hole.

Sekani, Chase, and Joseph jumped in beside the professor to help him pry off the rocks, but no matter how hard they tried, the rocks remained intact, as if they were cemented in place.

"I don't understand," said the professor as he stood, brushing the dirt off his hands and pants. "Kenyans are very protective and respectful of their ancestors. There is no way that they know about this grave. Otherwise, we wouldn't be allowed to excavate here.

"In all my years of teaching this course, I have never come across a grave," he said. He clambered out of the hole. "Let's cover it for now! Maybe we will have a better idea tomorrow, in daylight."

Sekani, Joseph, and Chase covered the hole with a tarp before laying rocks on each corner while the others went to tend to their bonfire.

*   *   *

She watched the sky turn red. Shadows stretched across the walls of her apartment. A tear slowly trickled down her cheek. With languid agility, he crossed the room, grabbed her by the waist and kissed her neck. He spun her around in his arms and searched her dark eyes deeply.

"Don't be so sad, Nera. She has been found. Soon we will be free . . . soon we will reclaim what is rightfully ours."

He kissed her passionately.

The sun disappeared behind the buildings, leaving them standing alone in the darkness, their silhouettes thrown against the crimson sky.

She walked away from him. She hated being watched, especially when it was time.

A dull, pulsing ache rushed through her body, followed by a burning sensation in her muscles. She gasped, clenching her teeth from the pain, and waited for the inevitable to happen; how she loathed this part of her life, the excruciating pain as she felt her bones snap and shift, forcing her to fall to her hands and knees.

She whimpered in agony, gasping for breath until the pain subsided to a dull throb followed by a most welcome numbness; an unnatural calmness overcame her.

The sweet scent of a baby drifted in the cool air. Its cry echoed in the night, mixed with the tantalizing aroma of human sweat. Her large black ears moved to the sounds flowing in the soft breeze from the open veranda.

She salivated from the smell, closing her mouth several times to swallow. There was a time when the strong, lingering smell of humans revolted her, but over time, her sadness transformed to anger and jealousy, and now the desire to sink her powerful jaws into the tender, delicate human flesh overpowered her.

Her mate jumped up and gently nipped at her ear. With the agility of a hyena, she tackled him to the ground, burrowing her face in his fur and gently squeezing her teeth around his jugular. She felt his strong pulse and released him only after he had surrendered, becoming submissive under her grasp.

She leapt off her mate, over the balustrade, and into the cold night, catching the scent of the others roaming nearby.

Her mate rolled back onto his paws and followed her.

Driven by the excitement of the hunt, they ran down the street before darting into the long grass to meet them.

*   *   *

"Good evening, Vanessa," Femi said to a dark, tall woman wearing beige coveralls.

"Hi, Femi! What brings you here today?" Vanessa grabbed a pair of gloves and walked over to a tall, metallic cage housing a wounded hawk.

"What happened to your hand?" asked Femi, noticing Vanessa's bandages.

"Oh! The mother chimp bit me when I got too close to her and her baby," she explained while pulling a glove onto her good hand.

"I saw Sekani the other day. Would it kill you to come and visit, or is it no longer convenient for you?"

"Vanessa, don't talk like that."

"Well, it seems like it. Now that he is old enough to take care of himself, who needs me?"

"It's not like that. We've been busy."

She entered the enclosure and placed her hand in front of the hawk's breast. Instinctively, the bird hopped onto her arm and began searching for the food Vanessa had hidden inside her curled fingers. It squawked at her loudly, flapped its wings, and bobbed its head up and down.

"What's got into you, girl?" she said, as she walked to the door of the cage that Femi was holding open for her.

"I hear that Sekani likes a girl at the camp. She sounds nice and very pretty," she added.

"Oh, yeah! Probably the blonde girl," he muttered, disapprovingly.

"Yes, Kathleen."

"It will pass."

"Is that how it is, Femi? Why don't you want this for him? He's happy. Is it because she is white?"

"No, that's not it at all," he said.

He followed her outside to a larger enclosure. She entered it, releasing her hold before the hawk flew to the nearest branch. Another hawk looked at it curiously while Vanessa exited the cage.

"And when were you going to tell me about Hanna?"

Femi took his hat off and brushed his short hair before donning his hat again. *Why do all the women I know feel it necessary to talk about things? Why does Sekani talk so much?* he thought.

Femi sauntered alongside the enclosures. Barks, hisses, and screeches resonated around the yard. He knelt near one of the fences and watched as a pack of jackals raced along the perimeters, jumping against the fence repeatedly. Some were jumping so high that they landed on their backs or sides before starting over again.

At another enclosure, a jaguar paced around the perimeter.

"Crazy, huh? It's like all the animals have gone mad," she commented, seeing that he wouldn't answer her question.

"I see what you mean," he agreed, feeling uneasy about the aggression these animals were displaying.

They reentered the small building.

"Look, even Sobek, our lazy Nile crocodile, has been grunting and hissing at the staff. That's not all—they're not eating," Vanessa explained.

She glanced at the front counter and noticed a box. She turned to face Femi.

"I should have known that you weren't here just to visit. What have you brought me this time?"

She walked toward the box and had gone to open it when he stopped her.

"It's a puff adder," he warned her.

"Why are you bringing me a puff adder?" she asked, knowing too well how one bite from this venomous snake could send a grown man to the morgue.

Vanessa backed away, leaned against the far wall, and glowered at him.

He knew she despised them, especially since one had claimed the life of her older brother when she was only a child.

"I didn't know where else to bring it," he answered.

"Well, this isn't the right place."

Femi could tell she was getting angry.

"I'm sorry. I know how much you don't like them," he said.

"That's putting it mildly."

"I just need to house it here for a couple of days before moving it to another place."

"All right," Vanessa relented. "Where did you find it?" she asked.

"By the school yard."

"Well, you know what to do!" She handed him a clipboard with an attached pencil and a form he was required to complete for each animal he registered at the sanctuary.

Nasiche Wildlife Sanctuary had been established fifty years ago by her parents. Now, she owned the sanctuary and managed a staff of five, who assisted her in caring for animals that had been injured, orphaned, or abused, or had lost their home due to habitat destruction. She was also responsible for their rehabilitation and the release of these animals into the environment.

Femi sat down and began writing the date, his name, the time, the location where the animal was found, the reason for registering it, and any remarks or observations that could assist her while it was in her care.

He handed her the clipboard. "How long have the animals been behaving liked this?"

"Well," she paused to think, "just today, before dusk. I've never seen anything quite like this before. It is almost as if they're frightened."

"Frightened?"

"Yes, come with me." She guided him through heavy doors to the home of a mother chimpanzee and her baby.

"Look at how she is rocking her baby. She's been sitting in the corner since nightfall. She's usually very friendly, but when I went to see her this evening, she didn't want anything to do with me, and when I came too close to her and her baby, well, she bit me," she said, holding up her bandaged hand.

"Do you have any ideas what could have triggered this behaviour?"

"Not at all. It's like they feel threatened by something—or someone."

"Did you want me to take a look around, to check things out?"

"Sure, if you don't mind. I would appreciate it."

Femi stepped outside. The cool breeze made him shudder. He usually enjoyed watching the sunset, but tonight, the crimson sky made him feel uneasy.

He walked over to the jeep, grabbed his rifle and flashlight, and began patrolling the area. There had to be an explanation for their behaviour: some of the animals exhibited aggressive behaviour, while the others showed signs of fear.

Half an hour later, he finished scouting the perimeter and had found nothing out of the ordinary. He returned his rifle to the vehicle and entered the small building, where Vanessa was preparing to close up for the day.

"Find anything?" she asked when she saw him enter the room.

"Nope! Nothing at all! Everything seems fine. Are you going to be okay tonight?"

"Yeah, I'll be fine."

"Let me walk you to your house."

"I live next door, Femi," she replied, her hands on her hips and her head cocked to one side. She straightened herself, softening her attitude. "Don't worry. I'll be fine."

"Okay, but at the first sign of anything, I want you to call me. I'll be on duty tonight."

"Okay," she agreed, flashing her brilliant smile. "Okay, now leave! I have to get this order ready for the morning, if I want to be able to feed everyone for the next six months," finished Vanessa before burying her head in her order forms.

Femi sat in the front seat of his jeep, recorded the time and place he had delivered the snake in his journal, and contemplated recording his observation of the animals' behaviour, but thought perhaps he was reading too much into it, and then drove away.

*   *   *

Everyone had attempted removing the stones, just in case one of them possessed some hidden powers that would enable them to move the rocks.

Kathleen sat beside the hole, staring at the grave and thinking about Sunjata. Okechuku joined her.

"So, what do you think is inside?" he asked.

"Huh?"

"What do you think is inside?"

"Probably nothing," she said. She didn't feel like talking. She felt sad and wanted to be left alone.

"Come on, Kat, you should join everyone by the fire," invited Sekani.

Kathleen looked up. She couldn't see his face, for the lantern's bright light blinded her. She and Okechuku got up, walked over to the fire, and pulled up two chairs.

Lost in her thoughts, Kathleen stared at the orange and yellow flames licking the wood.

"Hey, *Mzungu!* You okay?" asked Kianga.

Kathleen looked at Kianga, surprised.

"Yeah, I'm fine," replied Kathleen before turning in for the night.

CHAPTER 10

THE MCHANGA-MISITU WAR

Lying on her back inside her tent, Kathleen listened to the muffled sound of her friends talking, the fire crackling, and the occasional sound of someone walking nearby, unzipping his or her tent, and heading for bed.

Tears flowed whenever she thought of Sunjata. *But why does it hurt so bad? I hardly knew him. On many occasions, he told me to leave, but I didn't listen. It's all my fault.*

The next morning, she was awoken by a light breeze blowing in her hair and tickling her face and the sound of the opening of her tent flapping in the wind.

Kathleen bolted up. *Why is my tent open?* she wondered.

On her pillow, she saw a white flower. Its delicate petals fluttered in the breeze.

But who would have given me a flower? Sekani? Okechuku? She hoped it was Sunjata.

At breakfast, Kathleen daydreamed about Sunjata: the way he touched her hair, and the way her body reacted to the slightest touch of his soft hands. Confused, she didn't know whether she should forget about him and do as he ordered—leave—or go back and find out why he had reacted the way he did.

Kathleen exited the dining tent and stood outside to stare up at the mountain.

"Do you want to go spelunking again?" Okechuku stood beside her, looking up.

"No!" she replied.

Sekani, who had joined them, raised an eyebrow at Kathleen. "I thought you loved exploring caves."

"I do, but I've already explored most of it . . . and there's nothing. Come! Let's hurry before all the good spots are taken," she added quickly before walking toward the bus.

"You're telling me that you'd rather visit Kanzikuta Village?" Sekani said.

Kathleen looked into his eyes and lied. "Yes."

Sekani looked at the mountain. "Are you sure?"

"Yes," she said, grabbing his hand and leading him onto the bus. Her eyes met Okechuku's, and she registered the look of confusion on his face.

On the bus, Sekani slipped into one of the seats in the back while still holding Kathleen's hand. Kathleen escaped Sekani's hold, grabbed Okechuku's hand, and sat in the seat behind Sekani. Sekani was about to say something when Lisha walked up to him, flashing her bright smile, and sat beside him. Sekani glowered at Kathleen before sitting down with Lisha.

When the bus came to life, Okechuku laughed, for the bus jolted forward several times before coming to an abrupt stop. The bus bucked again before it sped forward at a high speed down the dirt road. He laughed even louder when he saw Kathleen cringing over the ear-splitting sound of grinding gears.

"Did anyone bring extra water and blankets?" he hollered and whispered to her, "I wouldn't be surprised if the engine fell out. Did you see the rust on this thing? Nothing is holding it together." He raised his voice again, asking, "So, Kat! Who do you think is in the grave?"

Kathleen looked at him. Sekani turned around in his seat to participate in their conversation.

"Njeri," she said dreamily, looking out of the window at the blurred landscape. A sudden jolt made Kathleen grab Okechuku's hand—the driver had swerved around a pothole, almost stalling the vehicle.

Embarrassed, Kathleen let go of his hand.

"Who's that?" asked Sekani. Okechuku and Sekani waited in silence while she continued to stare out of the window.

"I don't really know," she said without looking at them. She remembered the name from her vision in the library, but she still didn't know who she was or why all of this was happening to her.

Sekani sat back down in his seat.

The conversation had stopped after she had told them whom she thought the grave belonged to, which gave her plenty of time to ponder Sunjata. She had convinced herself that the flower was from him, and she fantasized about what he would say to her. She imagined being in a castle with him, overlooking a vast land.

The bus came to a halt, startling Kathleen back to reality.

As soon as they had exited, Chase and Joseph headed for the general store, while Adesina, Lisha, Amber, Sadia, and Tanisha sauntered over to the boutiques. Mrs. Sakala and Mrs. Standfort slowly walked to the general store, completely engrossed in their conversation.

"Professor," called Sekani as he grabbed hold of Kathleen's hand as she had done earlier and held her there.

Kathleen glowered at him.

"Yes, Sekani."

"Do you mind if we go to the Kanzikuta library? I would like to do some research about our site."

"Sure, as long as you're back here by, let's say, three thirty."

Sekani checked his watch. "Sounds great!" he agreed.

The professor walked toward the general store.

Kathleen struggled to get her hand free, but his hold was too strong. Okechuku walked over to Sekani and was about to say something when Sekani hollered at Kianga, who was lingering around the bus with her hands in her pockets, watching the girls shop at the different stores.

"Hey, Kianga! Do you want to join us?" he asked.

She turned around, surprised. She shrugged her shoulders before asking, "Where are you going?"

"The library," Kathleen said. Then she turned to Sekani. "You're hurting me."

Sekani let go of her hand.

Kathleen rubbed her hands together before looking up, surprised, when Kianga accepted.

"Why are we going to the library?" asked Okechuku.

"To find out about Njeri," he explained.

"Oh, no! You won't find anything about her there," said Kianga.

"You've heard of her?" asked Sekani.

Kianga shrugged her shoulders and looked away.

"Right!" Sekani muttered. Kathleen frowned.

"Where is it?" asked Okechuku.

"There," he pointed to an old, weathered wooden building. Part of the porch's roof had collapsed on its south side, preventing any sun exposure from the south.

"You're kidding me! It looks like it's going to cave in at any moment," he said.

"That's the whole idea," said Sekani, who looked at Kianga and smiled. She returned his smile and walked ahead of them. Kathleen and Okechuku looked at each other, puzzled.

"I guess they know something that we don't know," whispered Kathleen.

While Kianga marched ahead of them, Sekani explained that saying the name Njeri was strictly forbidden.

Several times throughout his life, he'd heard the name being whispered within some small circles of women living in secluded tribes in the area. When he had asked someone about it, he was warned never to speak of her. He'd been told that just mentioning her name may unleash an evil omen, for she was often blamed for the drought, disease, and famine in some villages.

"That's ridiculous," Kathleen said.

Inside the Kanzikuta library, Kathleen stopped; it was the library from her dream. The interior was in direct contrast to the outside.

Gleaming wooden floors stretched from the entrance to the back wall, where rows of book-laden shelves cast shadows along the floor.

"Are you coming, Kat?" asked Sekani.

Kathleen briskly walked past him and began looking down every aisle until she came across the one with the small window—the one from her dream, where the woman had cornered her.

Kianga frowned at Kathleen. "Looking for something?" she said.

Kathleen ignored her. She walked down the aisle to the window, looked down, and picked up a small wooden carving of an antelope. She placed it on the windowsill.

"What are you doing?" asked Sekani.

Kathleen spun around, bumping into Okechuku. She walked around them and began peeking between books, pushing them aside to get a better look at the room behind them.

"Are you looking for someone?" Sekani asked.

"No," she answered. "Who could I possibly be looking for?"

"I don't know, but you sure know how to scare someone, Kat," said Okechuku.

"Why do you say that?" asked Sekani.

"Because when Kat entered, a woman in the library saw her and scrammed out of here, running," he explained.

"Was she black, in her midthirties?" asked Kathleen.

"Good one, *Mzungu*! That's pretty much everyone here," remarked Kianga.

Kathleen, Sekani, and Okechuku searched through all the books they could find about the history of Kenya, while Kianga sat in a corner leafing through a magazine.

Sekani decided to get help. He walked over to the librarian, whose curly white hair framed his gleaming dark face.

"Do you have anything regarding the Mchanga-Misitu War?" Sekani asked.

"Sorry, son . . . everything we have is on these shelves," replied the librarian.

"Anything on Njeri?" asked Okechuku, who had joined him.

"Shhh!" hushed Sekani.

When they overheard Okechuku's question, Kathleen and Kianga joined them.

"Did you say Njeri?" whispered the librarian, seemingly intrigued.

"Yeah!"

Everyone turned to face him with excitement.

"How did you come to hear about her?" he asked.

Both Sekani and Okechuku turned to look at Kathleen, who simply shrugged her shoulders; she didn't like the sudden attention.

Sekani looked at her seriously.

"How do you know about Njeri?" demanded Sekani. "You can't possibly still believe that we don't know what's going on."

The librarian looked at Kathleen with keen interest.

Kathleen shook her head. She was not about to tell them and risk sounding crazy.

"Why do you want to know about her?" questioned the librarian. He looked at Kianga, who in turn looked shyly at the floor.

"We found . . ." said Okechuku.

"*We* found an amulet that may have belonged to her," lied Kathleen.

Sekani and Okechuku stared at her in astonishment.

"Good one," muttered Kianga.

"And do you have this amulet with you?" asked the librarian, leaning closer to Kathleen, who was starting to feel very uncomfortable.

"No, but I would recognize it in a drawing," she replied quickly, so as to not deter him from helping them.

"Well, we don't have anything here," he said.

Okechuku, who was really starting to enjoy this mysterious adventure, threw his arms up in the air in exasperation.

Sekani spun around, frustrated.

"What did I say?" said Kianga.

"Not here, but I know where you can find it. I'm not guaranteeing that it will be there, but it's worth a try," the librarian continued.

Kianga looked shocked.

Kathleen gave her sarcastic smile.

Sekani looked at the old man in disbelief as he hobbled over to the back room and hollered, "Nadia!" He then came back out and grabbed an old key that was hidden at the back of a drawer. A young black woman walked up to the counter from the back room. "Keep an eye on the place while I'm gone," he ordered.

"Yes, Mr. Galimi," she replied meekly.

The librarian led Kathleen, Sekani, Okechuku, and Kianga to the back of the library. They exited through the back door into a wall of heat. They walked past several old huts until they reached the last hut. Mr. Galimi furtively glanced around before opening the rickety wooden door. He held the door open for the teens and then closed it behind them.

They stood on opposite sides of the room. Daylight poured in through a small, square window, illuminating a large tapestry positioned in the middle of the floor. Against the far wall, a wooden crate with rusty old metal hinges was hidden in the shadows.

Mr. Galimi opened the wooden crate, took out two oil lanterns, and lit them before handing one to Sekani. He lifted the tapestry and tossed it to one side, exposing two wooden doors. He bent over and placed his fingers inside two holes where the doorknobs would have been and pulled the doors open. A loud creaking sound resonated in the small room, followed by a loud thud as the doors slammed against the floor

Narrow, stone-carved stairs led straight down into the darkness.

The librarian began to descend the steps, followed by Sekani, Kathleen, Okechuku, and Kianga.

Sekani had to hunch over in order to fit into the long, narrow tunnel at the bottom. Mr. Galimi didn't have that problem: from all the years of having to compensate for his bad leg, he hobbled, leaning most of his weight on his right leg; crouching was a natural state for him.

They entered a large, dark chamber where Mr. Galimi proceeded to light torches. The dank room felt instantly warmer, and the smell of the kerosene overpowered the musty odour.

Tall, dusty wooden bookshelves that housed thousands of old manuscripts and papyrus scrolls drooped under the weight. Some of the shelves had collapsed, trapping books and pieces of yellowed, dust-covered parchment underneath. Scattered paper covered the ground.

Mr. Galimi pulled out a large, dust-covered book strung together by thick twine from a stack of loose papers.

"I believe this is what you are looking for," he said.

Kathleen walked over to him. He looked at her and handed it to her. She lifted the cover. A shroud of dust swirled in the dim, flickering light. Kathleen coughed.

Sekani and Okechuku peered over her shoulders while Kianga sauntered around with her hands in her pockets.

"I can't read this. Are you able to translate this, Mr. Galimi?" asked Okechuku.

"I . . ." Mr. Galimi stammered when he heard Kathleen, beginning to read.

"680 BC, in a kingdom called Mashujaa Wa Mchanga lived a king named Jelani who married a beautiful woman, Akiki."

Sekani glanced over at Okechuku.

"How can she read this?" whispered Okechuku.

Kianga approached them, staring at Kathleen with disbelief.

"Do you want to hear this or not?" she scolded them before continuing. "They had fourteen children . . . I'm not reading all their names," she said, turning the page.

"Is there anything about Njeri?"

Kathleen glided her finger down the page before turning to another. Just when Okechuku was losing interest, Kathleen called out.

"Check this out."

Mr. Galimi brought the lantern closer and listened.

"Here, King Rapula, from the kingdom of Walinzi Wa Misitu, had nine wives; his most favourite was Queen Kosazanna, who bore him a son, Kokayi."

"But the children's tale speaks of two sons," said Sekani.

"Shhhh!" she hushed him.

"Sorry . . . continue."

"Six years later, the queen gave birth to another son, who she named Akono." "Great . . . is there more?" asked Okechuku.

"No, that's it," she answered.

Page after page, Kathleen read of how King Rapula conquered land and power. His army expanded as he conscripted men and boys, capturing their women and girls and making them into slaves.

"Here! I found something. It says that the youngest son, Akono, fell in love with a lovely woman, named Njeri. Right!" Kathleen said dismissively.

"What? Do you have something against people falling in love?" asked Okechuku.

"No, I don't, but I do have problems with history being warped and changed to hide the truth," defended Kathleen.

"And what do you think really happened, miss?" asked Mr. Galimi, who seemed to find Kathleen very interesting.

"I don't know," she answered, looking up at him.

Kathleen truly didn't understand why she had said that. It was as if they had been speaking about her, telling their version of her story and knowing very well that wasn't what had happened. Kathleen shrugged her shoulders.

"Best to keep your opinions to yourself, young lady. We take great pride in our history and culture," warned Mr. Galimi.

"Sorry, sir. I didn't mean any disrespect."

"I know, child. Does it say anything else, miss?" asked Mr. Galimi.

"It only says that the king died three years later from a bad heart. Nothing else was written here." She handed the book to Sekani before walking to the other side of the room. She glided her fingers over the spines of the dust-covered books and shuddered when she remembered her vision of the bleeding book. She remembered being frightened by it and hearing the words "Take it!" shouted. She stopped her finger on a green leather book. *Could this be the one?* she thought.

Kathleen pulled it off the shelf and examined it: a faded picture of a twisted tree, similar to the one at the campsite had been drawn on the cover.

She glided her hand on the symbols before glancing around.

While Sekani, Okechuku, and Mr. Galimi were speaking, Kathleen slipped the book inside her backpack, unnoticed by everyone—except Kianga. Kathleen glanced at her, afraid that she would tell, but Kianga kept her silence and nodded.

"Anything else?" Sekani asked, handing the book back to the librarian while Kathleen and Kianga listened from a distance. The librarian's translation was not as fluent as Kathleen's, for he had to pause several times to think of a word, or how to place it within a sentence.

"It goes on to explain how Kokayi became king of Misitu, but never married.

The thirsty earth . . . drought . . . brought on famine and disease. Death loomed over the kingdom . . . Kokayi ordered his brother, and his army of fifty thousand men to . . . march . . . through the savannah until they . . . got to . . . Nasiche Mountain.

"King Hundo, ruler of Mchanga kingdom, was great warrior and . . . powerful leader. At night, King Kokayi and his men attacked Mchanga kingdom, but Hundo had eyes on the mountain . . . soldiers guarding. They waited until they attacked before taking them . . . flanking them on all sides. The war went on for several moon cycles.

"That's it. It stops there," finished Mr. Galimi.

Sekani looked at the page and saw something scribbled at the bottom. "What's that say?"

Galimi squinted and brought his face so close that his nose almost touched the paper. "*Usiku ni kuangalia . . . jihadharini na kile uongo chini ya mchanga,*" Mr. Galimi looked up at the group.

"Can you translate?" asked Okechuku.

"The night is watching . . . beware of what lies beneath the sand," whispered Kathleen and Kianga simultaneously. They stared at each other, surprised and frightened.

"Kathleen, you're really starting to freak me out," said Okechuku.

"Starting? Didn't I tell you to stay away from that tree?" reminded Kianga, who was feeling a little uncomfortable.

"Don't start with the tree," said Okechuku.

"I wonder what that means," muttered Sekani.

"It means that since Kat banged her head on a rock, she's been acting weird, and now she can read—and probably speak—Swahili," explained Okechuku.

"It means you guys are messin' with stuff you shouldn't be messin' with," objected Kianga.

"Do you know who won the war?" asked Kathleen, ignoring their comments.

"That's the strange thing. No one knows what happened. Some say that on the third new moon, they vanished into the night, never to return," explained Mr. Galimi.

"Maybe it's like in Lisha's story," said Okechuku.

"That's just to scare children from going outside at night past their curfew," explained Kathleen.

"Most of our stories are based on truth," defended Kianga.

"So you're saying that the warriors turned to sand or are roaming the night as animals?" stated Kathleen.

"No, I'm just saying that—" said Kianga.

"Are we done here?" interrupted Mr. Galimi, who had suddenly become anxious to return to his library.

"Yes, thank you so much. You've been a great help," said Sekani.

"What time do you have?" asked Okechuku.

"Three twenty," answered Sekani. "Oh! We'd better go."

"Yeah, thanks," they said to the librarian before hurrying back to the bus.

CHAPTER 11

NJERI

"That was a waste of time!" said Kianga.

"Are you always this cheerful?" asked Sekani.

Kianga turned to confront him when she noticed him smiling at her. She turned her head and walked away in silence.

Sekani, Kathleen, Okechuku, and Kianga joined their group, standing by the bus.

Suddenly, out of nowhere, Kathleen felt a tap on her shoulder. She spun around to face the woman she had seen in the library in her dream.

"*Samahani!*" said the woman.

"That's the woman who left the library in a rush, Kat," Okechuku reminded Kathleen. "What did she say?" he asked.

"She said 'excuse me,'" explained Kathleen.

The woman grabbed Kathleen by her forearms and looked into her eyes.

"What is she doing?" asked Kathleen, nervously.

"It's okay, Kat! She's greeting you. Looks like she has something important to say to you," explained Sekani.

The woman let go of Kathleen's arms, reached down inside her bag, and pulled out a journal before handing it over to Kathleen.

"*Mimi na kitu ni lazima kuwapa,*" the woman said.

"I have something I must give you," Kathleen translated before Okechuku could ask.

"Am I the only one who can't speak Swahili?" Okechuku complained.

"Apparently," replied Kianga.

"*Kuchukua kitabu unataka mimi kuwa na hili?*" asked Kathleen.

"She said, 'I don't understand why you want me to have this,'" whispered Sekani to Okechuku.

"Not bad, for a white chick. She even speaks better than me," said Kianga.

The woman looked deeply into Kathleen's eyes and said, "Njeri."

Kathleen understood.

"*Asante,*" she thanked her.

The woman gave Kathleen a hard look before walking away. Kathleen thought the woman seemed nervous, almost frightened.

"Did I hear her right?" asked Sekani.

"Yeah! It's about Njeri," she said excitedly. "Njeri wants me to know this; that's why I've been having all of these dreams."

"Whoa, Buttercup!" said Kianga, wiping the smile off of Kathleen's face.

"She's right!" agreed Sekani.

Kathleen shifted her gaze from Kianga to Sekani. "You can't say her name, and especially don't tell anyone that you've been having dreams about her," explained Sekani.

"But . . ."

"Listen. In many regions of this country, just saying her name can buy you a one-way ticket to the afterlife, if you know what I mean. People associate her name with terrible things, and if they find out what you've just told us, you would be labelled a witch and persecuted."

"But what if she wants the world to know the truth? You've seen the history books; there is virtually nothing about her."

"That may be so, but let's not jump to conclusions before reading it, all right? Besides, you don't want that responsibility," whispered

Sekani, who was leaning closer to her while gazing into her eyes. He suddenly backed away in a hurry, turned around, and went over to stand beside Chase and Joseph.

Was he going to kiss me? she wondered. Confused about the recent events—and about Sekani—she waited quietly until they were allowed to climb onto the bus.

"Well, are you going to read it?" asked Okechuku.

"Let's wait until we get inside," she said while looking over at Sekani.

Their eyes met before Sekani quickly turned to speak to Kianga. Kianga's eyes drifted from Kathleen to Sekani, and a smile spread across her face.

The professor marched past the group, knocked on the bus door, and entered.

They followed, streaming to the back. Kathleen slid toward the window, accompanied by Okechuku.

Kianga sat behind them with Sekani.

Lisha, who saw the new seating arrangements, glared at Kianga.

The professor walked down the aisle, counting heads to make sure everyone was present before giving the driver permission to leave.

"How many dreams have you had, Kat?" asked Okechuku, concerned.

"Just a few," she answered.

"I think she's possessed," whispered Kianga.

They looked up to see Sekani and Kianga craning over their seat, watching them. Kathleen wondered if Kianga was standing or on her knees, as Sekani was significantly taller than all of them.

"Well, are you going to read the story, or should I?" asked Sekani.

"Okay," she said, defensively.

She opened the book. "Look, it's written in English," Kathleen noted before she began to read.

My name is Helen. This is not my story, but the story
first told by a courageous woman and then passed down

from generation to generation. It is a story that recounts a part of history that some wish to be forgotten.

I write this story in hope that the truth will find its way back to our people . . . and that she will be forever remembered as someone of great importance, and not an outcast, to be feared.

This is her story.

In a kingdom in West Africa lived the Walinzi Wa Misitu tribe. Milele Misitu, an enchanted forest, was home for the Misitu, but not by choice. Everyone knew that it was forbidden to live within the forest for any length of time greater than what was permitted. However, when the king died, his son Rapula took the throne and ordered everyone to make Milele their permanent home.

On a moonless night, the cry of a woman pierced the tranquility of the forest. Nada stepped outside of her home and listened. The cool breeze of the night swept across the land, rustling both the grass and the leaves on the trees. Something felt wrong, very wrong. An ominous silence lingered throughout the kingdom as Nada watched two women, servants of the king, stealthily sneaking in the shadows before entering deeper into the forest.

Curious, Nada followed them. She hid behind a shrub and watched as one of the women placed something on the ground before they retreated back to the castle.

Nada waited patiently for the return of the midnight chorus, but none ever came. The song of crickets she was so used to hearing was gone, and instead, a foreboding silence had spread across the land.

Nada walked slowly to the tree and knelt beside a small lump of clothing on the cold forest floor. She unravelled the clothes and gasped. She immediately hid the bundle underneath a raised root of a tree and hurried back.

At home, she woke her daughter and helped her get dressed before guiding her into the forest. She carefully retrieved the bundle and handed it to her.

"Apana, you must leave at once," said her mother.

Nada lifted the cloth to expose a newborn baby.

Confused, Apana looked at her mother.

"What's going on, Mama?" she asked.

"This baby was left to die. She's the king's daughter. You must take her far away from here and keep her safe. Follow the stream through the forest and into the savannah. Keep going straight and head for the mountains."

Tears welled up in her daughter's eyes. "But I don't know how to take care of a newborn baby!" she cried. "I have no food, no water."

"Do not worry, Apana," she held her daughter's face against her chest while tears trickled down her cheeks. "You will manage. Follow my directions and you shall find guidance."

"What about you? If the king finds out . . ." said Apana.

"He won't. You must never return, and I will mourn your death. Go, my child. Travel at night, for it will be cooler, and rest when you must, but not for too long: you have to keep moving," explained Nada.

They embraced. "I love you, Mama."

Apana ran into the dark, thick forest, the infant snuggled tightly against her chest. She heard the trickling song of the stream and followed its twisted path through the forest. *The river of Maisha will guide me*, she thought.

In the day, the trees sheltered her and the baby from the sun, and the creek kept her cool and hydrated. Unable to appease the infant, Apana sobbed, rocking the baby back and forth until eventually the infant fell asleep.

She had reached the line where the green forest met the golden savannah and waited for night before crossing. The cool night breeze heightened her senses as she stepped across the threshold into the tall silver grass. She ran for short distances, crouching low to the ground to make sure she wasn't seen or heard.

For most of the night, the child was silent. Several times, Apana feared that the infant had died, and felt relieved whenever it stirred and whimpered. Nonetheless, she was worried, for the baby's cries were becoming weaker and less frequent.

Day came with its blazing heat. Apana sat under the dappled shade of a tree. The baby slept on. Apana's worries intensified. Her stomach ached, and though she was used to surviving on an empty stomach, the pain was becoming intolerable. In tribes such as hers, only the royalty had the privilege of sating their greedy appetites. But the baby needed to eat, and without milk, she feared the worst. Apana started to cry.

On the third night, she saw the most unusual sight: fireflies, flashing brilliantly in the night, danced before her eyes. Apana followed the tiny light display until she reached a small, round clay house. She walked over to the door and jumped when the door opened, unexpectedly.

An angelic woman with delicate white skin that gleamed like the sand on a Kenyan coastal beach and hair as black and lustrous as a raven looked her over.

"We have been waiting for you, Apana," she said before she moved aside to let her in. "Please enter."

"How did you—" she began.

"Shhhh! Come in," interrupted the woman. "There's no time to explain. This baby must be bathed and fed, immediately. She is hungry and dehydrated."

Inside, the smell of earth, fresh rain, and herbs caressed her senses. The woman ushered the frightened young girl into a large, dimly lit room where the orange light from the stone fireplace danced on the earth-covered walls.

Intricate filamentous roots and branches cascaded from the walls and ceiling, seemingly used to dry herbs, plants, and other materials unknown to her. The moisture from the cool night air formed droplets that twinkled in the light as they trickled down the roots into large vases, capturing their essences.

The crackling sound of the fire, combined with the dripping sound of water, relaxed her.

The woman who had greeted her was an African beauty, whose dark curly hair glimmered in the light, accentuating her dark expressive eyes. She wore a long, red wraparound dress adorned with miniature beads.

An Asian woman wearing a long, silver silk gown adorned with blue flowers, her hair pinned up in an elegant swirl, was stirring something in a pot while it brewed on the fire.

"She is beautiful," said the African woman as she disrobed the infant. All the women gathered around the baby, admiring her tiny form while bathing her in cold water; the baby started to wail.

"What are you doing?" shouted the girl.

"This child needs to be woken and fed, or she will die. She's been sleeping for far too long, without getting the proper nourishments."

The Asian woman held a linen cloth open as the Caucasian woman handed the baby to her. She then wrapped the baby in the warm cloth.

When the baby was dry, the African woman sat in a chair and waited for the Asian woman to place the child on her lap. She immediately nuzzled the baby against her exposed breast, but the baby ignored it. The woman massaged her nipple and began excreting milk. She opened the baby's mouth and tried to coax it to suckle: the baby did not respond.

"She's not waking," she said, worried.

The Asian woman disrobed the infant and began dripping cold water on her back before lightly blowing on the baby's skin. The infant squirmed. The woman continued until the baby finally latched on, and began suckling. Several times, the baby fell asleep, but the woman continued stimulating her until she felt the infant had had ample to drink. While the baby slept, the Asian woman gave Apana something to drink.

"My name is Annika," she said, bowing to Apana. She then returned to her steaming pot.

"I'm Buseje," said the African woman, "and this is Madison." She nodded toward the Caucasian woman. Apana didn't know if it was the aroma in the house, her drink, or the way Buseje spoke, but suddenly she felt very sleepy. Madison guided her to a bed behind a small wall of hanging herbs.

"We are witches, and we are here to assist you. You are going to stay with us for a few days so that both you and the baby can regain strength," explained Madison. Her long, black hair brushed against her face while she helped Apana lay down.

"I can't take care of the baby . . . I don't know how," she explained. Her eyes were feeling very heavy.

"Rest, my child. You've done well. Do not worry about matters that are out of your control. We will speak more in the morning."

The next day, Apana awakened to feel a dull pain inside her breast. Panic-stricken, she had forgotten where she was. She jumped out of bed and ran from behind the wall to where she saw Buseje nursing the baby.

"Apana, did you sleep well?" she asked.

"Yes, but why do I hurt?" she crossed her arms over her breasts. They felt larger and fuller.

"Ah! The special tea Annika prepared you has already started to take effect." Apana frowned.

Buseje explained. "In order to take care of this child, you will need to nurse it."

Apana shook her head. "No . . . no . . . I can't," she said. Tears welled up in her eyes. She missed her mother, terribly, and she wasn't ready for this.

"Yes, you can, and yes, you will. This child's future depends on you, and so does the future of your people," she continued.

"I don't understand," she said. She sat down to listen.

"You must name her Njeri. It will be your responsibility to care for her and to teach her the ways of the world. The path she must follow has already been chosen for her. At the age of twelve, Njeri will be taken from you."

On the fifth day, Buseje, Madison, and Annika sent Apana and Njeri on their way. Apana was to continue traveling west, toward the mountains, until she came across a quaint little village, where the Nzuri Mahali tribe lived.

Two weeks later, Apana entered the Nzuri village.

To her surprise, she was welcomed with open arms. Later on in her life, she was married into the family where she raised Njeri as her own. As promised, Apana cared for her and lived a very full life.

Apana had forgotten what Buseje had said, and as forewarned, on Njeri's twelfth birthday, King Rapula and his men entered the village, conscripting the village's men and boys. Anyone who resisted was killed on the spot. One of the king's sons, Akono, took a liking to Njeri. When the king saw this, he ordered his men to take her.

Heartbroken, Apana watched helplessly as her daughter fought and screamed while one of king's men carried her away.

The village was pillaged and burned to the ground; the women were left sobbing, the children clinging desperately to their mother's dresses, afraid to ever let go.

Why does it have to be this way? Was it worth all the pain? I lost everything when my mother told me to take Njeri, and now I have lost everything again—my husband, my new family, and worst of all, Njeri, she thought. Crushed, Apana fell to her knees and cried.

Five years later, a wanderer entered the village. He had a message for Apana. She opened the piece of parchment and looked back at the messenger.

"Would you please read this for me?" she asked. The messenger took the letter, glanced at Apana with a stern look, and began to read.

Dear Mama,

I hope this letter finds you well. I have taught myself to read and to write.

I am married to Akono. I know that he loves me very much, and he takes good care of me.

Things have changed . . . and because they have broken the forbidden rule, it is with great sadness that I must tell you the forest you loved so dearly as a child is no longer.

Death surrounds us.

The king is dead, and Kokayi, Akono's older brother, is heir to the throne.

We are traveling east to find new land and to start over.

Remorse haunts me, and my hands cannot be cleansed. I fear that I will never lay my eyes upon your beautiful face again, in this life or in the afterlife, for I feel responsible for my father's death. I hope you can find it in your heart to forgive me. My destiny may have closed the door to the eternal life.

Love, Njeri

"Whoa! Do you know what she just admitted to?" asked Sekani.

"Yeah! It's like what they say—what goes around comes around," said Kianga.

"That's not funny," said Sekani.

"Who's laughing? It serves him right. Do you know how many innocent people died because of him? He got what he deserved," said Kianga.

"She changed the fate of life for her kingdom, gave them freedom. And what did she get for it? Nothing! Someone went to great lengths to slander her name and fabricate lies," argued Kathleen.

"That's what it seems like," agreed Sekani.

"But why?" asked Kathleen.

"So the king could remain powerful. Even to this day, he is spoken of as a great, formidable leader," explained Sekani.

"So, why is Kat dreaming of her?" asked Okechuku.

"Because in Njeri's eyes, the war is not over," concluded Kathleen.

CHAPTER 12

THE GRAVE

Back at the campsite, Kathleen was confused by what she'd learned about Njeri.

Was Njeri responsible for King Rapula's death? she thought.

While everyone was busy talking about the items they'd purchased in Kanzikuta Village, Kathleen glanced at Okechuku and Sekani to make sure that they were occupied with something other than her. Kianga was sitting by herself, whittling a stick.

Maybe Sunjata can tell me what happened to the king, and maybe now would be a good time to talk to him about our last confrontation, she thought.

Halfway up the path, she realized that she had forgotten her flashlight. Kathleen decided to continue on without it and proceeded up the path until she reached the cave entrance. She entered the cave, but remained in the sunlight. She heard footsteps approaching her from the darkness. Fear raced through her body. What if it wasn't him?

A set of yellow eyes glimmered before her.

"Sunjata, is that you?" she whispered timidly, staying in the sunlight.

"Yes, it's me," he answered softly.

She sighed.

"I'm glad you came back," he said. "I'm so sorry about yesterday. I had no right to be upset with you." His crouched silhouette appeared. He hid his eyes from the light with one hand, and extended the other hand to her.

"I don't understand why you said those things to me," she said, ignoring his advances.

"I'm afraid for your safety, Kathleen. I thought by saying these things to you, it would make you want to leave. I don't want to see anything happen to you," he answered.

When she took his hand, a wave of excitement overcame her.

He led her carefully into the dark.

"There is so much I want to tell you, but the less you know, the safer you are," he explained.

"But, Sunjata, I know about her," her voice trailed off when she felt his finger against her lips, making her forget the purpose of her visit.

He held her against him.

"Why do you keep coming?" he whispered in her ear, his lips lightly brushing against her earlobe; his hot breath tickled her skin, overwhelming her with a wave of elation and dizziness.

"The same reason why you want me to come back," she replied.

"I'm sorry, Kathleen."

"Why?"

"For messing with your head. This could never work, between us."

"Can you explain to me why you . . ." She stopped talking when he kissed her forehead.

"I can't explain. It's too complicated. I'm not doing us any favours by having you here. All I know is that it's not safe for you."

"I know. You keep saying that. Anyway, I have to go before someone notices that I'm gone."

"How could you ever go unnoticed?" he said. He guided her by the hand back to the entrance. All of a sudden, he withdrew his hand.

"Is everything all right?" she asked, concerned by his sudden change in behaviour.

"Yeah . . . didn't realize how late it was getting . . . you're right . . . you have to go," he said between breaths.

"Okay," she said, hesitantly. Kathleen began to walk towards the crimson light when she spun around. "Oh! Sunjata!" she called out.

"Ye . . . e . . . e . . . ah!" His voice came in short gasps from deeper inside the cave before she heard him inhale deeply.

"I'm pretty sure that I found Njeri's grave," she explained. She wondered if he was still there.

There was no reply until a muffled whimper resonated in the dark.

"Sunjata! Are you all right?" she asked, worried.

"Go!" He shouted. "I'll see you tomorrow," he added quickly. His tone wavered, becoming hoarse.

"You sound like you're in pain," she said with concern.

"Don't worry! Go!" he whispered while panting heavily.

She exited the cave. *What was that all about?* Lost in her thoughts, she sauntered down the path, oblivious to how dark her surroundings had become.

Suddenly, someone grabbed her by the arm, spun her around, and covered her mouth before she was able to scream.

"Be quiet," whispered a voice she immediately recognized; it was Sekani. He released his hold of her while he searched the darkness.

"What are you doing?" she whispered.

"Saving your life," he said.

"I don't need . . ." her voice faltered when she heard an ominous growl.

Two forms leapt before them with shining red eyes; she couldn't tell at first what they were.

The sound of claws scraping a nearby boulder alarmed her. She glanced quickly toward the sound and saw red eyes staring down at them from above, their bodies' silhouettes against the red sky.

"Hyenas!" she squealed.

Sekani grabbed her hand. *"Jump!"* he shouted.

"*What?*" she screamed while he pulled her down the mountainside. They slid along the steep slope in complete darkness while small avalanches of sand and rocks buried their shoes and branches whipped at their faces.

Sekani dropped on his back, knocking Kathleen down with him. Two hyenas had jumped on the rocks before them, blocking their escape.

Without taking their eyes off the hyenas, Sekani and Kathleen clambered back up the steep hill. They froze when they heard cackles and barks coming from above. They were trapped. At that moment, a loud roar pierced the night.

Sekani held Kathleen tightly against him, protecting her.

Barks, cackles, hisses, and roars resounded in the darkness, followed by whimpers, yelps, and screeches.

They ran full-out before finding their way to the campsite. Huffing and puffing, they both stopped and bent over, gasping for air. A stitched of pain ripped through Kathleen's side.

A deafening shot rang out through the night.

"*Come!*" He grabbed her hand and ran past the vehicles to a man who was aiming his rifle into the darkness and moving his sight in sync with his target.

"*No, not the lion!*" shouted Sekani.

The man lowered his rifle and glanced at him; it was Femi. Without uttering a word, he sprinted away from the camp into the night, followed by Lucas and Moses.

"Wait, Father!" Sekani shouted. He guided Kathleen over to Okechuku before chasing after him.

"Are you okay?" asked Okechuku, holding Kathleen by the shoulders.

"Yeah, I'll be fine," she replied. She slipped out of his hold and bent over to catch her breath. Her legs were shaking.

"What were you thinking, going into the night?" he asked.

"It wasn't night when I left," defended Kathleen.

"Yeah, don't forget how much closer you are to the equator. The sunset doesn't last long in this country," he said. "Good thing Sekani's dad showed up when he did. Otherwise you—"

"Okay, okay, I got it!" she interrupted. "You don't have to hover over me."

"Is that what you think I'm doing?" he asked. A hurt look flashed across his face.

Kathleen looked up at him.

"You know, I was all wrong about you, Kat! I thought you cared, but now I know the only person you care about is yourself." Okechuku walked away.

"Oke! Oke!" she called after him before straightening herself. *Could this evening get any worse?* she thought.

Femi, Sekani, Lucas, and Moses returned.

"Are you guys all right?" asked Professor Holdsworth.

"Yeah! They're far from here, now . . . gave them a good scare," Femi said between breaths before turning to Kathleen.

"May I ask this young lady what she was thinking? You almost cost me the life of my son," he said.

"No, it wasn't her fault. I wanted to show her the cave. I didn't realize what time it was. I'm the one to blame, not her," Sekani defended.

Kathleen stared at him in disbelief.

The professor threw his arms up in the air and walked away. "All right, everyone! The show is over. Get back to the fire!" he hollered before muttering, "I'm getting too old for this."

"Sekani, a word!" Femi commanded. Sekani and his father sauntered toward his jeep.

Kathleen joined the group by the fire. She looked across the circle of teens and saw Kianga sitting beside Okechuku. He gave Kathleen a scornful look before glancing away.

Kianga looked at her and shrugged her shoulders.

Now Kianga seems to be on my side, she thought. *But why did Sekani do that for me?* She glanced away and stared into the night. The bellow of a lion echoed in the distance. Her thoughts drifted to Sunjata. *Who is he? Why does he stay alone in that cave, and why didn't he come to our rescue?*

Her thoughts were interrupted when Sekani sat down beside her.

"My dad will be staying at the campsite tonight," he said. He watched his father lean against the jeep, holding his rifle in the crook of his arms while searching for shadows in the savannah. The professor joined him.

Sekani looked at Kathleen when the chatter around the fire became louder. "We need to talk."

Kathleen rolled her eyes and sighed. *What now?* she thought. They moved away from the fire, and Kathleen saw Okechuku glaring at her.

"Promise me that you will not go to the cave without me," he said.

Kathleen glanced away. She knew it was a promise she couldn't keep. How could she promise him that when all she wanted was to be with Sunjata?

Sekani grabbed her face and made her look at him. "Promise me," he demanded.

When she didn't reply, he released his hold and walked away, frustrated.

Kathleen marched over to her tent, unzipped it, and entered. She changed into her pyjamas, slipped inside her sleeping bag, and stared at the ceiling. Feelings of remorse crept deep inside her. She felt touched that Sekani had come to her rescue, but why couldn't she stop thinking about Sunjata? She knew how Sekani felt about her. It was quite obvious, with the glares she was getting from the other girls. But something about Sunjata lured her to him—and now her two best friends were angry with her.

* * *

Vanessa sat in her kitchen. A cool breeze blew in through the open window, making her shudder.

She poured herself a cup of tea, opened the door, and sat on the steps of her porch. An ominous silence fell around her. She listened for the sounds of her animals, but there were none to hear. She got up, opened her door, grabbed her flashlight, and quietly closed the door behind her.

The gravel crunched with every step as she approached the back gate. She could hear a clinking sound. Vanessa stopped to listen. She flashed her light through the gate—nothing. The hinges squeaked when she pushed the gate open and entered the sanctuary.

The soft hoot from an owl welcomed her; its little yellow eyes peered at her from the darkness. The clinking sound, followed by a whimper, alarmed her. She spun her light around and crept forward, slowly. She thought she heard something coming from behind her, so she quickly turned her head and searched the shadows with her light, but found nothing. She continued walking until she reached the jackal's enclosure. A jackal slammed against the fence before collapsing to the ground; its blood-matted fur gleaming in the moonlight. She saw another dog lying on its side, whimpering.

"What could have done this?"

She peeked around the corner and was surprised when her light fell upon freshly dug earth; a gaping trench spanned the width of the fence.

A low, growling rumble came from behind her. Vanessa froze. The hair on the back of her neck stood up. She felt sick to her stomach as she turned around, slowly. Her heart sank when she saw six pairs of red eyes staring at her, their lips curled back into smiles, exposing their sharp teeth. Vanessa reached for her cell phone and gasped; she had forgotten it on the kitchen table.

This was not the way she had envisioned her life ending.

*   *   *

Sheltered inside the jeep's heavy canvassed cab, Hanna and Lee watched the pride through a small opening, using their night vision goggles, while Hunter recorded the night events on film. The silver grass glistened in the moonlight as the lionesses stealthily stalked a small herd of zebras.

The herd's alpha male lifted its head, rotated its ears, and froze. Simultaneously, the harem followed its actions. The male stomped its hoof and barked, alarming its harem before galloping toward the lions hidden in the grass.

"What startled them?" asked Hunter.

"Shouldn't they be going the other way?" asked Lee, watching the zebras leap over the crouched lions.

"Keep filming. We're about to find out," said Hanna, staring into the night.

They watched in silence as a clan of hyenas emerged, circling the pride.

Teeth bared, they attacked one by one, sinking their powerful jaws into a tail or a leg. The incessant cackling and snickering of the hyenas sent shivers down Hanna's spine as she watched the lions try to defend themselves. A male lion came charging; it lunged forward, sinking its powerful claws into a hyena's back. The hyena fell to the ground before hurrying back up.

"This is horrible. I've witnessed the animosity between lions and hyenas before, but usually it's to scavenge," said Hunter. "We can't just sit here and watch this."

"We can't interfere. We are only here to observe," reminded Hanna.

"But this is not normal. This is just malicious," protested Hunter.

"Check this out!" shouted Lee.

Hanna peered through her binoculars at the lions while Hunter continued filming.

The hyena's matriarch stopped. She stepped away from her clan and looked in their direction. Others of the clan joined her and stared at them. Silence returned.

The pride disappeared into the night.

"That's freaky," whispered Lee. "It's like they know that we're here."

"That's not possible!" said Hanna.

"I think they're coming for us," said Hunter.

"But how?" asked Lee, who was continuously adjusting his binoculars as the hyenas got closer.

"I don't know, but I think you should start the engine," said Hanna. Hunter stopped filming and climbed over to the driver side before dropping his equipment on the passenger's seat. Lee and Hanna watched the clan as they separated, flanking the vehicle on all sides.

A hyena slammed against the passenger-side window.

"Did you see that?" he yelled, fumbling with the keys.

"Hunter, we should get going!" cried Hanna. She grabbed a flashlight and turned it on.

A hyena jumped on the hood of the jeep, climbed up to the roof, and began clawing and tearing at the canvas rooftop. Another started to tear the canvas at the back.

"I'm trying—I dropped the keys," he replied, searching the floor with his hand.

Hanna dropped her light on the floor and grabbed the fire extinguisher. She began slamming it against the hyena's head as it tried to squeeze its muzzle through the torn canvas.

"Lee, go help Hunter find the keys," she ordered. "I give them five minutes before they have the whole roof ripped into shreds."

Lee jumped to the passenger side, pushing aside the film equipment He leaned forward and began hammering on the horn—nothing.

Two hyenas were now pulling and ripping at the canvas near the front windshield. In the back, Hanna began throwing random objects at a hyena that had managed to squeeze partially through the tear.

She opened a storage container and pulled out a rifle. She grabbed a tranquilizer dart, opened the latch, and loaded it. But before she could close the latch, the hyena jumped on her, making her lose the dart. She swung the rifle to her left, knocking it hard, but the hyena overpowered her. She fought, holding its snarling muzzle away from her face with the rifle, while she glanced around for the tranquilizer dart that had fallen out of her reach. She spotted the red tail of the dart sticking out from underneath a fallen coat.

The hyena snapped its powerful jaws at her, pushing hard against her; its muzzle was inches away from her face before it stopped. It looked from her to the dart lying on the cab's floor.

"No, you don't," she said as the hyena leapt off her. Hanna rolled under the animal towards the dart and grabbed it before plunging it into its stomach. The hyena landed on her, pinning both of her arms down. The animal looked at her and smiled before descending its powerful jaws toward her face. Hanna closed her eyes and felt its sharp teeth touch her forehead and upper lip before it suddenly went limp, collapsing on top of her.

Gross! The animal's saliva wet her face and lip.

The jeep jolted forward, knocking one of the hyenas off the roof.

Hanna rolled the hyena off her and began kicking at another hyena at the back at the truck, when it grabbed hold of her leather boot, crushing her foot with its powerful jaws. Hanna screamed. She fell to the floor and began kicking it with her other foot, trying to free herself.

Lee clambered to the back and began hitting the head of the animal repeatedly with the butt end of the rifle.

"Get the tranquilizer!" she hollered.

Lee grabbed a tranquilizer dart from the case and stabbed it into its neck. Soon, the effects of the drug took hold, and the hyena dropped to the floor, its body hanging partially outside the canvas.

While Hunter drove away, Lee assisted Hanna with the medical kit. She removed her boot and doused her bleeding wound in isopropyl alcohol.

"Ahhhhhhh!" she screamed in pain.

Lee grabbed bandages and wrapped her foot tightly.

The truck stopped. "I think we're safe," said Hunter. He turned around to look at them. "What in the world just happened here?"

"I don't know," said Hanna.

Lee grabbed the flashlight and walked over to the animal.

"Hey guys, have you ever seen a hyena like this before?"

* * *

The night had transformed the savannah into a myriad of greys. Kathleen walked toward Babu Mountain, which towered over a sea of silver grass swaying in the slight breeze. The silhouette of the twisted tree remained untouched by the wind, as if it were a painting hanging against the backdrop of Kenya.

From the corner of her eye, she saw movement. A tall, black woman strode past, her long, black dress and veil billowing to one side. The woman stopped, looked back, and signalled for her to follow.

Kathleen trailed behind her. The mysterious woman vanished in front of the tree.

She was walking over to where the apparition had disappeared when her foot slipped. Kathleen stepped back, catching her balance. She glanced down and saw the woman she had been following lying inside the grave. A black leather sachet hung around her neck, and through the slit of the woman's dress, Kathleen caught the glint of something metallic wrapped around her leg.

Kathleen began tossing and turning in her sleep. Her dream transformed; now, she was running. She tripped and fell to the ground. A hyena stepped over her and whispered her name.

She sat up in her bed, drenched in sweat.

"Njeri!" She heard the name spoken aloud, as if her nightmare had followed her into reality.

Grunts and whimpers echoed in the night. She got up, unzipped her tent, and stepped outside. In the dim moonlight, she saw a multitude of silhouettes racing around their dig site. She walked toward them and noticed that the shadows were a clan of hyenas, scratching and pulling at the tarp in a frenzy. Unafraid, she approached them, removed the rocks from each corner and slid the tarp off. The hyenas jumped onto the grave and began clawing at the rocks before urinating on them, eroding the adhesive that cemented the rocks together. The hyenas then jumped out of the hole and ran away into the night.

Kathleen jumped down into the grave and removed several stones. A sliver of grey light lit up the small opening she had created. Inside, a black mist seeped from the earth and slithered above the skeleton's chest, solidifying into a black leather sachet. She reached in and pulled out the leather pouch she had seen in her dream before returning the rocks she had moved. She then walked back to her tent, lay down, and fell fast asleep.

The next day, she removed her pyjamas; dirt had stained her pyjama bottoms, and a foul stench reeked from them. After she got dressed, she unzipped her tent, stepped outside, and stretched.

Okechuku noticed her and looked away.

"What a sight for sore eyes, if you ask me," said Sekani. He gave her a toothsome smile.

"What time is it?" asked Kathleen, as she rubbed her eyes and yawned.

"It's eleven o'clock," he answered. "Come see what happened."

He grabbed her hand and led her to the pile of rocks. They squeezed through the throng of teens standing around and looking at the contents of the grave. Once inside the circle, she saw Joseph, Chase, Amber, and Adesina finishing up with the removal of the last stones.

Sekani stood by and watched.

Everyone stared in silence.

Inside the grave, they saw skeletal human remains. The skull of an animal had been positioned on top of the human skull.

"Who do you think it is?" asked Amber.

"I don't know," answered the professor.

"What's that?" said Chase, pointing to the light reflecting off a partially exposed piece of metal.

"It's her dagger," said Kathleen before jumping down into the hole.

"Her!" huffed Adesina. Everyone started to laugh, except for Okechuku, Sekani, and the professor.

She dusted off the sand around the skeleton's left thigh, grabbed the handle of a dagger, spun around, and stabbed it into the ground outside the hole before stepping back out of the grave.

She loved the way everyone stared at her in awe, moving aside and giving her space as she confidently pulled the dagger out of the earth and marched away—especially the concerned looks she saw on the faces of Sekani, Okechuku, the professor, and, surprisingly, Kianga.

Sekani watched her go before glancing at Okechuku and Kianga.

"If you're so smart, who do you think this is?" Lisha shouted after her.

Kathleen turned around, annoyed. "It's Njeri, of course. Anything else you want to know?" she asked before she proceeded to the dining area, a smile stretching across her face, satisfied with the comments she overheard.

"How could she know about Njeri? Isn't she from Canada?" she heard Lisha ask.

"Can anyone explain to me what's going on here?" The concern in the professor's voice only amused Kathleen.

"What's happening to her?" she heard Okechuku asked.

"Njeri's back," Kianga replied.

Kathleen couldn't agree more.

Later in the afternoon, Kathleen watched the professor, the doctor, and the translator carefully remove Njeri's remains. One by one, the bones were positioned onto a long, rectangular wooden board before being wrapped in a white linen cloth. As Kathleen watched them carry her bones to the professor's truck, a sense of relief and exuberance washed over her.

CHAPTER 13

NASICHE WILDLIFE SANCTUARY

The call he'd received at 6:45 a.m. from one of the staff members working at the Nasiche Wildlife Sanctuary worried him. It wasn't like Vanessa to leave her home unlocked or the gates to the sanctuary open. Something was wrong, and he still had an hour and forty-five minutes of driving before he would arrive.

Already, the heat thermals radiated off the hardened, parched earth. Femi slammed on his brakes. He opened the glove compartment of his jeep, took out his binoculars, and stared through the oculars into the vast sea of scorched grass.

"What the heck?" he said. He stepped hard on the gas, spinning his tires on the light dirt before turning the steering wheel hard to the right. He traveled off-road, bouncing violently around as the jeep sped across the rough terrain, slowing down after he had reached his destination. Femi hammered on the brakes, making the jeep slide forward before coming to a complete stop. He sighed heavily.

The vehicle's shredded canvas swayed in the breeze, and the cracks in the windshield reflected the sunlight.

Femi grabbed his rifle from the back of his jeep, loaded it, and opened the door. He stepped out and circled the perimeter of the other vehicle before pulling on the driver's door handle. The door swung opened; it was empty. He cautiously walked to the back and opened the tailgate. He clambered inside, holding onto his rifle firmly. Equipment, wires, broken glass, and papers were scattered across the floor.

In the corner, he spotted dried bloodstains and a first aid kit that had been left open, its contents strewn on top of its lid. He examined the tattered canvas before jumping out. "What happened here, and where are they?"

On the sand, he noticed boot prints. He climbed into his jeep and began driving slowly, following the tracks. After traveling ten miles, he found them; they were heading toward a remote village. He drove up to them and stopped.

Hanna spun around and limped over to him before throwing herself into his arms.

Surprised, Femi held her, comforting her while he watched Lee and Hunter standing in the distance, looking exhausted.

"Sorry," she said, wiping the tears from her eyes. Lee and Hunter approached them.

"What happened? I saw what's left of your truck and then followed your tracks here."

"We were monitoring the pride's activity last night, when . . ." Hanna paused.

". . . when we were attacked by a clan of hyenas," finished Lee.

"Hyenas? How?" asked Femi. "What happened to your foot, and your truck?" asked Femi, pointing back in the direction he'd come from.

"There were six or eight of them. They attacked our truck, and one bit Hanna's foot," explained Hunter.

"I don't get it," he said, thinking about the hyenas he had chased away the night before.

"They weren't your ordinary hyenas, either. No, these were smart," said Lee, tapping his finger on his temple, "and larger than your average hyenas."

"I don't understand," said Femi.

"Femi, these hyenas knew where we were. They came directly for us." Hanna rubbed her forehead with the sleeve of her shirt. "I've never seen anything like this before. I think we've discovered a new species."

"A new species?" asked Femi.

"Well, we were able to tranquilize two of them, but the hyenas were having a bad reaction to the tranquilizer," explained Hanna.

"They were going into cardiac arrest," added Hunter. "So we had to give them a shot of epinephrine to counteract the drug."

"But that's not the weird part," explained Lee, excitedly. "When the hyenas were under the effects of the tranquilizer, something was happening to their bodies."

Femi looked even more confused.

"The fur was thinning out, and—" Lee paused to catch his breath.

"What?" Femi looked from Lee to Hanna and then to Hunter.

"Femi, I think if we hadn't intervened, the hyenas would have died and transformed into something else," said Hanna.

"Transform? Hanna, that doesn't make any sense," said Femi.

"I know it doesn't, but I know what I saw—I mean, what we saw." Hunter and Lee nodded in agreement.

"Another thing . . . you know how hyenas are capable of hunting in the day, as well as in the night," she said.

"Yeah!" he agreed.

"Well, these were completely nocturnal. They cannot stand daylight—or any light, for that matter," she explained.

"Then we have the advantage. Let me give you a ride to the village, but first I have to stop by the Nasiche Wildlife Sanctuary," said Femi. He scooped Hanna into his arms and carried her around to the passenger side of the jeep.

Lee and Hunter smiled, ran to the jeep, and slid into the back seat. "I have water and some snacks in the cooler."

Relief and excitement flashed across their tired faces. "Thanks."

It wasn't long after their departure that they had eaten their fill and Lee and Hanna had fallen asleep.

Femi looked back and noticed that Hunter was still wide-awake. "Not tired!"

"I don't understand what happened. I can't shake it from my mind. It's like having watched a horror movie; the only difference is that we were part of it. I've never been this terrified in my life," he admitted.

The jeep bounced from one pothole to the next. Femi looked back again and noticed that Hunter had finally drifted to sleep.

Fifty minutes later, they had arrived. The two tire paths he followed were fringed by tall golden grasses, which whipped the vehicle as it drove through. Gnarled acacia trees stretched open toward the sky, begging for a refreshing rainfall to quench the land, and give it life, once again.

A large wooden sign with Nasiche Wildlife Sanctuary painted in black swayed on small metal chains; it marked the entrance to the sanctuary. Femi parked near the front of the main building, where he had been just hours before.

A black woman in her early thirties wearing a long yellow dress with her hair securely wrapped in a yellow cloth walked over to them.

The passengers stirred in their seats.

"Where are we?" asked Hanna in a groggy voice.

Femi stepped out of the vehicle before he could answer.

"Teshia, has Vanessa returned?"

"No, sir. I don't see her since last day before I go home, sir," she said.

"Do you mind if I look around?" asked Femi, even though he had entered the premises many times before without need of an invitation. Everyone knew him and liked him, but this time if felt different: Vanessa was missing.

"I do not mind, sir," she said before reentering the white building.

Femi looked at the occupants inside his jeep. They were slowly waking. "I'm going to have a look around," he said to them.

The door opened, and Hanna jumped out.

"And who is this Vanessa?" she asked.

Hunter and Lee clumsily stepped out to stretch their legs.

"She's a friend and the owner of this sanctuary. Shouldn't you be resting?" he added when he saw her wince in pain.

"Don't worry about me. You seem worried," replied Hanna.

"It's not like her to just leave."

Femi marched over to a small house, which was beautifully decorated with flowering shrubs and vines. The others followed him silently. The wood creaked when he stepped on the back porch. He walked to the door and opened it.

"Vanessa!" he shouted. He heard his companions' footsteps resonating throughout the house.

He searched every room for any sign that may explain her whereabouts while Hunter and Lee stood in the entrance, watching. Hanna looked in the kitchen.

"Femi, she left her cell phone on the table," Hanna called out.

Femi returned to the kitchen to where she was standing.

She handed the phone to him.

The display indicated that she had missed three calls—all messages he had left this morning while attempting to reach her.

"She's not here," he muttered.

Panic-stricken, Femi stepped back out into the sunlight. Hanna and her teammates followed. Femi quickened his pace. He walked over to the back entrance to the sanctuary. The gates had been left wide-open. "That's strange! Why would she have left the gates open?"

They entered.

He marched toward the back of the building while Lee and Hunter walked alongside the enclosures.

"Hey, guys! You should come and see this," called out Lee, who was standing by the jackals' cage.

Femi ran over to him while Hanna slowly limped towards them. All the jackals lay dead inside the enclosure; a large hole had been dug up from beneath the chain-link fence.

"What do you think did this?" asked Hunter.

"I don't know, but my guess is that Vanessa must have heard something and came outside to investigate. Whatever did this . . ." Femi voiced trailed off.

Femi saw Hunter look at Hanna with concern.

"What's wrong?" Femi asked him.

"Do you think that maybe the species of hyenas that attacked us last night could have been responsible for this?" asked Hunter, rubbing the back of his neck with his hand. He continued when he saw Femi frown at him. "I've found hyena tracks," he muttered, pointing at the ground near the enclosure and looking uncomfortable with the situation.

"*Vanessa!*" yelled Femi. He began to run from enclosure to enclosure, searching the ground alongside the fences and behind the shrubs at the edge of the sanctuary. Nothing.

"*Vanessa!*" he called out again. It was then he spotted something in the shrubs ahead: a piece of shredded clothing dangled from a branch. He held it up for the others to see.

Hanna rushed over to him. "That could belong to anyone," she said, trying to reassure him.

Femi shook his head. "She was wearing this when I saw her last night."

"Guys!" shouted Lee. "I found a flashlight."

Femi ran over to him, grabbed it, and began examining it. "That's hers. Where did you find it?" he urged.

"Against those shrubs over there," Lee said, pointing.

Femi searched under and inside the shrubs but found nothing. Choked up, Femi kneeled in the dirt, paralyzed by a fear and a reality that was much too fresh in his mind. Old wounds of a loss so unbearable—he thought he had locked them away for an eternity— had resurfaced. Pain he was unable to deal with gripped him at the heart—all she had wanted was his friendship.

"Femi," said Hanna, placing her hand on his shoulder. "She probably had to go to the village. She's probably fine," she said, trying to comfort him.

Femi looked up into her eyes and nodded. *She was right. I have to remain focused. I will find her, and everything will be fine,* he thought. He pushed his emotion aside as he'd done for so many years and stood up.

"I'd better get you to the village," concluded Femi.

"What will you do?" asked Hanna.

"I have to get my son," he said. "If what you're saying about the hyenas is right, then they are heading for the campsite."

"Well, I'm going with you."

"Same here," agreed Lee and Hunter.

"You said that they are completely nocturnal?" he asked.

"Yeah!"

"Great! That buys us some time. Perhaps we should stop at the general store."

Lee and Hunter looked at him with curiosity.

"We'll need flares, and I might as well check to see if I've received my fax from Constable Whitmore."

* * *

Kathleen glanced away from her book to see if she could catch a glimpse of Sekani. To her dismay, he was sitting across the campsite, looking directly at her. *Why is he like this?* All day, she had wanted to visit Sunjata but couldn't—not as long as Sekani was keeping a close eye on her.

Sekani gave her a smile.

She smiled back and returned to her textbook. The professor wanted everyone to read chapter 10, "The History of Archaeology." They only had four books in circulation amongst a large group of eleven teens, and it was her turn to read.

"Are you almost done, Kathleen?" asked Professor Holdsworth.

"Almost," she answered, sifting through the pages to see how many were left. Kathleen signed. "I still have five pages."

"Good work! When you're done, pass it on to Sekani."

At the mentioned of his name, he smiled and waved at her. Kathleen turned her back to him.

* * *

Femi entered the Kanzikuta General Store and found old man Binah restocking the shelves.

"Hey, I knew I smelt foul air when I came in this mornin'," he grumbled.

"Did you get a fax for me?" he asked.

"Ah! Let me see," he said, getting up from where he was working before opening the door to the back room and disappearing inside.

Ten minutes later, he reappeared with a stack of papers, closed the door behind him, and slowly shuffled his way over to Femi.

"What's this about?" he asked while handing him the documents; had Binah known how to read, he would have read them.

"Just business," he replied.

"You call what you do a business?"

"How much do I owe you?" asked Femi, placing the documents down beside a box of flares, some matches, and a tin of lighter fluid.

After paying him, he walked out of the store, opened the hatch to drop off the box of items, closed the door, and sat in the jeep.

"Did you get everything you needed?" asked Hanna.

"Yeah! Check this out." He handed her the reports.

Hanna leafed through the stack of papers. "What am I looking for?"

"The cause of death."

"All were caused by lions?" she asked. "That's hard to believe." Hunter and Lee leaned forward in their seats to have a look.

"Can I see?" asked Hunter. Hanna handed him the reports.

"That's what I thought," Femi agreed.

Femi dialed a number on his cell phone.

"Hey, Rick. It's Femi. Good. Yeah, it's been a long time," he said. "I need a favour. I need you to find out what you can about Dr. Mekufa. Anything. Okay, thanks a million. You got my number? Good, talk to you soon!" He placed his cell phone down.

"Who was that?" asked Hanna.

"A good buddy of mine. We went to school together in Embu. He now lives in Nairobi."

"Do you think this has anything to do with last night's hyena attack?"

"I don't know, but something is not adding up. We have coroner's reports all indicating the cause of death to be lions, and here we have three separate attacks by hyenas," explained Femi. "Let's get back to the site. I have a strong feeling our hyenas will be making an appearance." Femi started the engine and backed the vehicle up before driving off south.

After having his turn at reviewing the reports, Lee handed the papers to Hanna.

While driving, Femi's thoughts drifted to Vanessa. Since Sandra's death, he had made the decision to never get close to anyone for fear of losing her. He pushed Hanna away when he first met her, and with Vanessa, he had kept his distance, visiting her whenever he thought Sekani needed a mother figure.

Now, she could be gone—and he had never taken the time to thank her and tell her how much she meant to him.

The cell phone rang; Femi switched the phone to speaker mode.

"Femi here!" he shouted over the engine's rumbling noise.

"Femi? It's Dr. Blackwell."

Femi looked at Hanna while Lee and Hunter listened intently.

"How is the investigation coming along?" asked Femi.

"Not good . . . no time to explain. I just got a call from Professor Holdsworth. A grave was found at the archeological site, and inside there were the skeletal remains of a human."

"They what? When? I was just there this morning," said Femi.

"One of his students believes that the remains belong to Njeri. Apparently, she found a dagger head with lazurite embedded in the grooves," she explained.

"Who found it?" asked Lee.

"I believe it was Kathleen Gallant," answered Dr. Blackwell.

"Isn't that the blonde girl your son has taken a liking to?" asked Hanna.

"I'm afraid so," he confirmed.

"Femi?" said Dr. Blackwell.

"Sorry, Dr. Blackwell. I have Hanna, Lee, and Hunter sitting here with me. So, what are you saying?" asked Femi.

"I'm saying that the student who found her body and dagger is in great danger," she explained.

"I'm heading for the campsite right now."

"That's good! Be on the lookout for lions!"

"I understand why you think that the lions have been killing archaeologists who dug up artefacts from the Mchanga-Misitu era," said Femi.

"That is correct."

"Well, Hanna and her teammates are biologists, and they were just attacked by a clan of hyenas," said Femi.

"Oh, really?" she said before pausing.

"Dr. Blackwell?" Hanna called out over the engine's noise.

"Yes, dear!"

"I don't know if this information will be helpful to you, but two of the hyenas that attacked us, when under the effects of the tranquilizer, were going into cardiac arrest, and it seemed like they were transforming into something else."

They waited in silence for her response.

"Are you there, Doctor?" asked Femi.

"Yes, I am. Were you able to determine what they were transforming into?" she asked.

"No, we gave them epinephrine to counteract the drug," she explained.

"I see. Thank you for sharing this with me. I'll be heading over to the site as soon as I can."

"All right, see you then!" said Femi.

* * *

In the distance, Kathleen saw a black spot on the horizon; a shroud of dust swirled in its wake. Sekani stood up as well and watched as the familiar jeep sped in their direction before coming to an abrupt stop and covering the professor's vehicle with a layer of sand.

Four doors opened, and Femi, Hanna, Hunter, and Lee stepped out, looking exhausted and worried.

Sekani and the professor walked over to the newcomers.

"Father, is everything all right?"

Femi took off his fedora and wiped his forehead with his handkerchief. Hanna leaned against the jeep, Lee looked past the curious teens, and Hunter stared at his feet, avoiding everyone's stare.

"Yeah, things are fine. We've decided to stay and camp here for the night," said Femi.

"What's going on?" asked Sekani.

Kathleen watched him.

"Can you help me?" he asked, walking over to the jeep. He opened the hatch.

"Adrian, know how to use one of these?" asked Femi.

The professor looked up and jumped when Femi threw him a rifle. He caught it with both hands.

"I guess I could, if I need to," he answered, nervously.

"Trust me, you'll need to," he replied with authority.

"Hunter?"

"Yeah, I'm here," he answered, ready to catch a rifle.

"Lee?"

Lee caught the weapon with his left hand.

"Hey, don't I get one?" asked Hanna. Femi looked at her. "Just because I'm a woman doesn't make me incapable of handling a weapon. Just give me one," she ordered.

Femi handed her a rifle and then proceeded to distribute a box of shells to each of them.

"Do you mind telling me why you think this is necessary, especially around the children?" asked the professor.

"Who are you calling children?" asked Tanisha.

"Don't we get weapons?" shouted Joseph.

"Because . . ." said Femi, guiding the professor away from prying ears and ignoring the glares he was receiving from his students.

"Because a clan of hyenas attacked Hanna and her teammates last night, and I suspect that hyenas were responsible for the attacks at the Nasiche Wildlife Sanctuary."

"Is everyone all right?" asked the professor.

"They lost eight jackals, and Vanessa is missing."

"That's not good."

"I believe they are heading this way, Adrian."

"I thought we were on the lookout for lions. According to Dr. Blackwell—"

"Yeah, I know what she said," interrupted Femi.

"Could the hyenas that were here a few nights ago be from the same clan?" asked the professor.

"I don't know. It was too dark to tell."

"What about my class? We have to send everyone home," said the professor.

"It's nightfall in four hours. Hanna said that these hyenas don't like the light, so we are safe during the day. We need to create a wall of fire."

"The heck with that! Why don't we just pack it in? We have two vehicles," argued the professor.

"There's no way we can accommodate all the students, the staff, and the crew," Femi explained.

The professor looked back at his class, frustrated. He returned his attention to Femi. "What do you want us to do?"

"We need to surround our site with large bonfires so that everyone inside is protected by the light, and we need a doctor to look at Hanna's foot. One of the hyenas bit her."

"All right!" he agreed. The professor turned around and began shouting orders. "Can I get everyone's attention? We need all of you to collect as much wood as possible for tonight. I need Sekani, Chase, Joseph, and Okechuku to get into the truck. We're going north where we'll find lots of dry wood," explained the professor.

Kathleen's eyes widened. She looked up; her eyes met Sekani's. He glared at her before walking over to Femi and Hanna. He then whispered something to them in private and turned to look at her, scowling.

"Dr. Racine?"

"Yes, Professor?"

"Can you please tend to Hanna's wound?"

Hanna's head perked up when she heard her name.

The doctor immediately rushed over to her side before guiding her to the nursing station.

Everyone was busy chattering to each other, wondering what the excitement was all about.

Kathleen watched as the truck drove away and took the opportunity to sneak up the mountain. On her way to the path, Femi confronted her.

"Going somewhere?" he asked.

"No," she lied.

"How are you feeling?"

"I'm fine."

"It's very nice up there, isn't it?" he said, trying to make conversation.

"It's all right. I'm going to go to my tent now, if you don't mind," she said. She knew that this was Sekani's doing.

Disappointed, Kathleen entered her tent. She sat on her makeshift bed, grabbed her backpack, and pulled out the book she had stolen from the library.

Kathleen tried to open it, but she couldn't. It was like all the pages were glued together. She sighed in frustration and threw it down.

CHAPTER 14

THE ORDER

"What do you mean, Njeri's body has been found?" shouted King Romani, his voice thundering through the large chamber. He held his staff high above his head while towering over his kneeling tribe.

Sunjata stood before his grandfather, with his head bowed and his hands on his chest to symbolize honour and respect while he waited for his decision.

The silence's cold embrace weighed heavily upon him; only the annoying sound of water trickling deep inside the rocks undermined the seriousness of this congregation.

King Romani's yellow eyes narrowed. He glared at the carved stone walls in frustration before pounding his staff on the hard ground. He stopped to look at his people.

Patiently, they waited for their grandfather to speak.

"You know what you must do," he finally said.

Sunjata's eyes winced at his words as if he had been flogged by an invisible whip. He looked at the king.

"Is there another way?" he asked, knowing very well that his grandfather could not be swayed.

"No! There is no other way to stop the Misitu warriors from rising and lifting the curse from their people. Do you realize what would happen, should this power fall into their hands? Our culture, our ways, and our freedom would be gone.

"It is unfortunate that so many innocent people have to die every year, but the Misitu tribe have been following the doctrines of a king that has been dead for over two thousand years. To this day, he remains extremely dangerous; King Rapula and his army must be stopped, at any cost.

"In all these years, never have the remains been found, especially someone of such importance. Therefore, it is most important that the person who discovered Njeri is killed," concluded the king.

Sunjata's heart sank; he was torn between the feelings he had for Kathleen and his loyalty to his family.

"May I ask who, Sunjata?" asked a tall, elderly man who had been standing beside the king. His pensive eyes seemed to understand the turmoil Sunjata was now faced with.

"I know who it is. It's that white girl Sunjata's been hanging out with," accused Sade, who gracefully sauntered past Sunjata, pushing him back to stand before King Romani.

Sunjata stepped forward to Sade's side. "Kathleen is only a young fifteen-year-old girl who came to Kenya to admire and to learn about our country. She means no harm," defended Sunjata.

"Sounds like Sunjata found himself a girlfriend," she remarked.

"That will be enough!" shouted King Romani.

Sade bowed her head to her grandfather. "Please forgive me for my rudeness, Great One, I meant no disrespect," she said. "May I ask you a question?"

The king sighed. "Yes, Sade."

"Truly Sunjata's mind has been clouded by his feelings for the girl. He is not thinking clearly. May I have permission to kill her myself?" she requested.

"No!" shouted Sunjata. He glared at Sade.

She glowered back at him, her lips slightly curled back. The dim lights flickered in her feline-like eyes. Sunjata understood that she was unable to comprehend. Family always came first, and to confront the king's decision was absolutely unheard of and unacceptable.

"And what would you recommend, Sunjata?" King Romani asked.

Sunjata stared at the king.

"Permission to carry out your orders, Great One."

Out the corner of his eye, he saw Sade's head whip around to look at him in disbelief.

"Permission granted. You are dismissed."

King Romani descended from where he stood and exited the cave, but not before stopping in front of Sunjata. He placed a hand on Sunjata's chest—a gesture of deep respect—before he left the chamber.

Sade walked over to the creek that trickled through the cave and sat by the water.

"Sade," greeted a king's messenger.

Sade stood up and bowed her head.

"The king has asked me to relay this message to you: Keep an eye on Sunjata, and make sure that he follows through with his task."

"Yes, sir," she replied.

*   *   *

Kathleen and Sekani were sitting quietly around the charred fire pit when they heard Okechuku shouting.

"Sekani, look!"

Sekani sprung up immediately, tipping his folding chair over. A vehicle in the distance was approaching quickly. An old, rusted pickup truck came to a stop before two black men jumped out; one man leaned back against the jeep, looking toward the campsite, while the other man leaned forward on his arms on the hood and watched.

Kianga reluctantly walked over to him.

"Come on, little sis, I don't have all day!" shouted the man before spitting on the ground.

Sekani, Kathleen, and Okechuku watched as others gathered around to see what all the shouting was about.

Kianga handed him a bag.

The man snatched it from her hand and examined its contents before throwing it back at her face. Kianga looked down. The man then grabbed her by the arm and lifted her off the ground.

"Let go of me!" she said, squirming.

Kathleen saw Sekani rush by her. "Sekani!" she shouted.

"Mr. Kaita! Mr. Kaita!" hollered Okechuku.

Immediately, Femi ran out of the tent. He looked at Okechuku, who was pointing to where Sekani was racing to. He reached inside his jeep and pulled out his rifle before marching over to Sekani.

Hanna, Lee, Hunter, the professor, and his staff joined the students.

They watched Sekani charge at the man who was holding Kianga.

At the sight of Sekani, the other man ran over to his brother's side.

The man shoved Kianga to the ground before taking a swing at Sekani. Sekani blocked him and then drove his fist hard into the man's gut. The man crouched forward, gasping for air.

The other man was about to jump Sekani when he heard the sound of a rifle being cocked. Both men looked up at Femi before backing away.

"You haven't heard the end of this, little sis," he cursed before jumping into the vehicle. The other man entered the pickup truck, slammed the door shut, and sped away.

Kianga got up and ran to the campsite.

"Kianga, are you all right?" asked Sekani, as she ran past him.

Kianga stopped, spun around and shouted, "Thanks a lot! Why don't you keep your nose out of other people's business?" She then marched over to her shelter box and disappeared inside.

Kathleen could see that Sekani was taken aback by her reaction.

"She had this," said Hanna. She handed a bag to the professor.

The professor opened it. "What's all this?" he asked as he pulled out a watch.

"Hey! That's my watch," said Chase.

"Hey! These are all of our things!" shouted Okechuku.

Several of the team members searched through the pile and grabbed what belonged to them.

"She's a thief!" cried Joseph.

A loud chatter broke out before Professor Holdsworth silenced them. "That's enough. I'll handle this. What's done is done, and I'm sure it won't happen again. There has been enough humility here."

He walked over to her sleeping quarters and knocked on the wooden frame. "Kianga, may I have a word?"

Due to the limited size of the shelter box, the professor had to kneel at the entrance in order to see Kianga. Ten minutes later, the professor painfully stood and left the shelter box, followed by Kianga, who felt embarrassed and didn't take her eyes off her feet.

"Kianga would like to say something," said the professor.

"I'm sorry," she said.

"Why did you do it?" asked Okechuku.

Kianga shrugged her shoulders and looked away.

"What happened to your hand?" asked Sekani.

Kathleen saw that Kianga's hand was badly blistered.

She turned to Kathleen. "Sorry, Kat. I tried to steal your dagger, but when I touched it, it burned my hand. I'd stay away from it, if I were you," she warned before she was crowded by a group of girls wanting to see her hand. Shocked by their reaction, Kianga looked at Sekani, who mouthed to her, "It's okay."

Kathleen turned away from everyone. *I held the dagger many times. Why didn't it burn me?*

Suddenly she looked up. The sky had darkened. A loud clap of thunder shook the ground.

She heard screaming.

The wind tugged at her shirt while a light rain fell upon her face. She blinked hard, letting the rain wash over her face for a moment until she was overcome with anger. She opened her eyes but all she saw where shadows. Driven by an inexplicable force, she marched to her tent, retrieved Njeri's dagger and leather pouch, and proceeded to climb the path up Babu Mountain until she reached the highest ledge.

A sense of power and exhilaration overcame her. She raised her dagger and pouch over her head and looked at the sky. The wind and rain whipped at her face and clothing while visions flooded her mind with memories and feelings of betrayal and remorse.

At first, she watched the story unfold, but soon the feelings overcame her, making her believe she was remembering a past more than two thousand years ago. Njeri had now overpowered her.

King Rapula stood before her. He crossed the dimly lit room to sit on a bed.

"Come," he ordered.

A candle flickered in the corner of the room. Reluctantly, she walked over to him. The king grabbed her by the arms, spun her around, and threw her on the bed, pinning her down. Njeri struggled to get free, but the king's weight and strength conquered her. A cruel smile stretched across his face.

Suddenly, Akono barged in.

Caught off guard, the king jumped up.

Akono pulled his dagger from its sheath, marched over to his father, and plunged his dagger into his chest. He then pulled it out and watched the king stumble back, clutching at his chest and staring at Akono in disbelief.

Kokayi entered the room.

Tears welled up in her eyes as she saw the king—the man who had abandoned her at birth, who had destroyed so many lives—fall to his knees. A surge of pity touched her. As the king fell forward, he grabbed the end table, knocking over a leather book before he fell sideways on the ground, staring at her.

Njeri stared at the book. She remembered hearing the servants talk about it, and apparently no one was able to open it.

While Kokayi and Akono were discussing what to do next, she crawled on her hands and knees and grabbed the book. She then looked at the king. His eyes were wide-open as if he were frightened as they gaped at the book.

Njeri crawled to the king, clutching the book against her chest. The king reached out and grabbed hold of her hands while gasping for air. The king opened his mouth to say something, but a gurgling sound was all that was heard. His eyes bulged as he slowly reached for it.

"Do you want this?" she asked him.

Njeri leaned closer to the king and searched his eyes before speaking. "How does it feel to be left for dead, Father?" she whispered.

With those words, the king's eyes widened as he struggled to breathe. "King,
you are no more. Never will you kill again; your days of destroying the lives of others are over."

Njeri turned around to face Akono. "I want the ashes from his heart."

He frowned at her for a moment and then agreed. "As you wish."

She sank to her knees, her hands smeared with his blood, and opened the book.

* * *

With her arms raised towards the sky, Kathleen shouted an incantation, awakening the sands, summoning both her ancestors and her nemesis, and staging Babu Mountain as the place to end the Mchanga-Misitu War.

The wind and rain continued to lash at her while she spoke. The thunder roared, and lightning flashed across the sky.

The teens had taken shelter in the dining area of the camp. The professor and his staff watched the storm from the entrance while the kitchen crew stared at the sky in horror, huddled together inside their unstable kitchen.

The tents flapped wildly in the wind. Sekani was sure that they were going to lose everything. He looked around and saw Okechuku and Kianga.

"*Where's Kathleen?*" he shouted over the wind and deafening downpour.

"*I don't know!*" shouted Okechuku.

Kianga shrugged her shoulders.

Sekani ran out into the storm.

"*Sekani!*" shouted Femi before following him outside.

Sekani looked around, but the rain blinded him. Suddenly as fast as it started, it stopped.

"*There!*" shouted Femi. Sekani looked up and saw Kathleen holding her arms high above her head. A bright light reflected off something she was holding in her hand before she collapsed on the ledge. He ran up the path, followed by Femi, Kianga, and Hanna. When he reached her, he picked her up. He was about to grab her dagger when Kianga stopped him.

"Don't touch!" she shouted. "Here." She said before pulling out a rag from her back pocket and grabbing the dagger.

"Good thinking!" complimented Sekani.

Femi carried an unconscious Kathleen down the mountain and took her to the nursing station.

"What happened to her hair?" asked Okechuku.

"I don't know," said Sekani.

The clouds dissipated, and the sun stretched its warm rays over the wet ground.

Dr. Racine ran to Kathleen, followed by the professor. She began examining her.

"Poor girl! She's really had a rough go since she got here."

"Will she be all right?" asked Femi.

"She seems fine, but she won't wake up."

"Why is her hair black?" asked the professor.

"I don't know," the doctor answered.

Kianga glanced at Okechuku and Sekani before waving for them to follow her outside.

"What's up?" asked Okechuku.

"You want to know what made her hair black?" she asked.

"Do you know?" asked Sekani.

"It may be difficult for you to understand, but if that skeleton really is Njeri," she explained, pointing toward Njeri's grave, "then I believe Njeri may have taken over Kathleen."

"Do you mean she's possessed? Are you serious?" Okechuku asked nervously as he paced, brushing at his hair with both hands.

"If that's true, what do we do?" asked Sekani.

"I remember my mother showing me how to make a draught to expel an evil spirit," said Kianga, a hurt look flashing across her face.

"I thought you didn't have any parents," remarked Okechuku.

Sekani glared at him.

"I did, *Mzungu*—before they were murdered. Happy now?"

"Oh, I didn't mean to—"

"Don't worry about it, but don't mention it again, or I'll have to knock your lights out," she warned.

Sekani laughed, and Kianga soon joined him. Okechuku chuckled nervously.

"Can you make the draught?" Sekani asked.

"No, I don't have any of the ingredients," explained Kianga.

*   *   *

In the nursing station, Kathleen tossed and turned in her sleep.

"Kathleen," said the woman wearing the black veil and dress. "Free me from my imprisonment. Set me free."

Kathleen woke up for a brief moment before falling back asleep.

CHAPTER 15

THE KILL

The next day, she woke up in the nursing station. She smiled when she saw Okechuku and Sekani sleeping on the ground beside her bed in their sleeping bags.

Kathleen sat up, and Okechuku stirred from his sleep.

"Hey, you're awake," he said in a groggy voice.

"Shhh!" She pointed at Sekani, who was still sleeping.

"How are you feeling?" he whispered.

"Good! Are you still mad at me?" she asked.

"No. How can I stay mad at you?" he replied. "You gave us quite a scare. What happened?"

"What do you mean? I was just about to ask you why I'm back in here again," she said.

"You don't remember climbing the mountain in that freak storm?"

"No, I don't."

"You're not going to like this," he said.

"What?"

"Take a look at your hair," he said.

Kathleen flipped her long hair over her shoulder to examine it. She smiled.

"That's how it was when we found you," Okechuku explained.

"It's okay, Oke," she said.

"It is?" he said, surprised.

"I kind of like it."

"Do you want to look in the mirror?" he asked.

"Sure." He retrieved a mirror he found on the doctor's makeshift desk and handed it to her.

She stared at her reflection and smiled. A beautiful black woman, whose curly, dark hair complemented her sparkling, brown eyes, smiled at her.

"Is everything all right?" he asked.

"Yeah . . . just admiring my new look," she said, handing the mirror back to Okechuku after taking a final glance at her reflection.

"If you like your hair colour that much, you should have dyed it years ago," he remarked. Kathleen could sense he was feeling uncomfortable.

Sekani woke up. "Ah, you're awake. You're all right, Kat?" he asked Kathleen. "Why didn't you wake me?" he said, nudging Okechuku as he stretched. "Did he tell you about your hair?"

"Yeah!"

"You must have got hit by lighting. You're lucky to be alive, Kat," he added.

Kianga walked in. "Hey, Buttercup," she said, and then paused after glancing at her hair. "I'll need a new nickname for you," she added.

Kathleen smiled.

"You seem different," said Sekani.

Kathleen shook her hair at him.

"No, besides your hair. You seem . . . more relaxed, like you don't have a care in the world," explained Sekani.

"Why shouldn't I? I mean, what else could happen to me?" she asked.

Okechuku nodded. "She's got a point."

"Anyhow, you don't have to worry. Good things are about to happen," she confirmed.

"Care to divulge these things? Because while you've been lying there, we've been going out of our minds," Okechuku said in a raised voice.

"It's time," she said and smiled.

The doctor walked in. "Okay, everyone! It's time to let Kathleen rest up," announced Dr. Racine.

"I think I need the rest more than she does," Okechuku said as he walked out.

"What did she mean by 'it's time'?" asked Sekani.

"Yeah, like I said—Njeri has unfinished business," reminded Kianga.

Suddenly, the sound of a car approaching and a very frightened kitchen crew caught their attention. Moses. Tsimba, Leticia, and Lucas were speaking very fast in their native tongue while piling into the car. The professor walked over to them, and shook their hands before closing their door. He stepped back and watched the car drive away.

* * *

The cool breeze swept through the opening of the nurses' station. Hanna slept on the cot beside Kathleen with a rifle at her side. She turned her back to Kathleen, pulled the blanket up to her neck, and continued to sleep.

Kathleen opened her eyes and slipped out of her sleeping bag. She grabbed a warm sweater and jeans and then walked outside. Sleepily, she was sauntering over to her tent when she came face-to-face with a male lion. The lion stepped forward and roared. Kathleen dropped her clothing and had begun to back away when something caught her attention: a lioness appearing from the shadows behind the lion. The lion followed Kathleen's gaze and roared at the lioness. The lioness circled the lion, keeping its distance and hissing.

From the darkness emerged four hyenas. They, too, began circling the felines, cackling and flashing their enormous teeth.

The lion charged forward at a hyena while the lioness kept low to the ground, getting ready to attack. The clan laughed and continued to taunt the felines, taking turns nipping at them from behind before running away with their tails between their legs.

The majestic lion roared ferociously as it helplessly spun around, charging and clawing at the hyenas while they evaded his attacks. The lioness jumped on the back of one hyena, but it quickly managed to get away. The incessant cackling grew louder when a hyena bit the lion on the shoulder. The lion caught one of its attackers by the leg and swung the hyena through the air. The hyena hit the ground forcefully, and then stumbled onto its feet and ran out of the lion's reach before returning to the onslaught. The lion roared.

The lioness managed to escape by leaping onto the professor's truck.

Kathleen continued to back away. She turned and was running toward Babu Mountain when the lioness leaped from the truck, landing behind Kathleen. She turned around and saw the lioness getting ready to pounce on her. Gasping for air, she ran as fast as she could. The lioness jumped on her back, its weight knocking the wind out of her. She covered her head with her hands and closed her eyes.

A loud shot rang into the night, deafening her. The lioness collapsed on top of her, its weight pinning her to the ground.

The lion and hyenas quickly scattered, disappearing into the night.

The smell of animal, blood, and gunpowder sickened her. All of a sudden, she felt the lioness's weight change; it was getting lighter. Kathleen turned over onto her back. Dark hair tickled her face, and an arm brushed against her hand. Kathleen screamed as she struggled to get out from under the body.

Femi ran to her and stopped, dropping his rifle. He fell to his knees and vomited.

Disoriented, Kathleen stumbled forward. Her ears rang, and the smell . . .

She ran into the cold night, trying to escape the images of the dead young woman and the smell of death. She wiped her arms repeatedly, trying to rub off the sensation of the woman's hair and warm skin. Kathleen dropped to her knees and threw up. On her hands and knees, she looked up and saw five hyenas standing before her, waiting.

* * *

"Kathleen!" shouted Sekani. He had begun running after her when Femi grabbed him by the waist, knocking him down. Sekani looked into his father's swollen red eyes.

"Don't go," Femi whispered, holding him tightly.

Sekani reached for him and hugged him. "I'm not going anywhere."

Hanna, Lee, Hunter, and the professor watched in silence. The other campers slowly emerged from their sleeping quarters, afraid of what they had heard and confused by what they saw.

Hanna immediately walked inside the tent, grabbed a blanket, and was about to cover the dead young woman's body when she noticed the dead woman's eyes change from a black, pearlescent colour to brown. Hanna closed the woman's eyes and pulled the cover over her face.

A lion bellowed three times into the night before an uncomfortable silence fell upon them.

* * *

Kathleen woke up on the cold, hard ground. Bewildered, she got up on her hands and knees and began searching around in the darkness.

"Kathleen," echoed a voice.

Kathleen jumped.

"It's me, Sunjata. It's all right. You're safe."

"Where are we?" she asked.

"You're in a cave, a few miles away from your friends."

He led her to the entrance of the cave, looking away from the sunlight, before retreating into the shadows.

"What happened?" she asked.

Sunjata didn't answer. Kathleen sat in the hot sun by the entrance; her shivering subsided.

"The woman that died . . . I recognized her. It was your sister, Sade," she said, trying to piece together last night's events.

"Yes, it was," he confirmed.

"But why?"

"I was given the order to kill you, but she must have sensed that I could not follow through with it," he explained.

"You were going to kill me! But why?"

"I was given the order by my grandfather, King Romani. For millennia, my family has been guarding the sands, and we have been successful . . . until you came along."

"Wait . . . you mean your family is responsible for killing all those innocent people who had found artefacts?" she said, feeling sick to her stomach.

"Yes, but only when necessary; the Misitu have killed indiscriminately."

"The Misitu? What does that have to do with anything?"

"Kathleen, you don't understand."

"No, I don't . . . and maybe I don't want to," she said as she started to walk away.

"Kathleen!"

She turned around. "Why didn't you kill me?"

"Because I fell in love."

He was standing in the sunlight, wearing the sunglasses she had brought him that dreadful day, when he had sent her away, crushed. His svelte, muscular chest gleamed in the light, and deep lacerations caked with dried blood stained his shoulder.

"I don't blame you for hating me, Kathleen."

"Why do you want to kill me?" she asked.

"I don't."

"But your family feels the need to."

"Because you discovered Njeri's grave," he explained.

"So?"

"I'm sure you can tell me . . . or she can," he stated firmly.

"What are you talking about?"

"Njeri is with you as we speak," he said, confidently.

Kathleen smiled. Her posture transformed to someone more relaxed, more mature and the colour of her eyes changed from blue to dark brown— almost black.

"And that frightens you?" she said.

"Ah, Njeri . . . you're back," he replied.

Njeri walked closer to Sunjata.

"Did you expect me to remain silent while my father's power continues to grow and to influence his faithful followers, infiltrating and poisoning the minds of our people?

"My mother didn't sacrifice her life for nothing. She knew I had a destiny, and it was to free my people from my father."

"What really happened that night?"

"Well, you knew that my mother Kosazanna died giving birth to me and that my father, King Rapula, was so angry that he had ordered his servants to get rid of me."

"No, I didn't. So, King Rapula was your father."

"Little did he know," she continued, "when he took me from my adoptive mother, Apana, when I was only twelve, he had, in fact, taken me back into the family. How ironic that the very man who left me for dead was in turn betrayed by his own blood."

"You killed your father, but history states he died from a heart attack."

"*Don't call him my father!* He was nothing to me!" She paused. "I was responsible for his death. I changed the future, and what do I get? Lies. What do they call me? An evil omen. A plague. How dare they?"

"What happened to all of us?"

"You want to know why you are cursed," she said. "I remember it like it happened only yesterday. It was a cold night, and the moonlight shone on the battlefield. I was watching from the shadows as King Kokayi and my husband, Akono, surrendered to King Hundo.

"Akono loved me. It was very difficult for him, though. I knew that I was his sister and could never be the wife he wanted. I loved him as a brother, and this made him feel incompetent as a man. Nevertheless, he loved me and cared for me."

"Did he know?" asked Sunjata.

"Did he know that I was his sister? No. I watched my two brothers surrender before the king when all of a sudden Kokayi picked up his blade and killed Akono. Little did I know that Kokayi secretly loved me. With Akono dead, he had hoped to take me as his wife. But he didn't expect me to be there, witnessing his murder of my husband, my brother."

"I'm sorry, Njeri."

"After my father died, I took something from him—a book. At the time, I didn't understand the importance of this book, but I soon realized that the king was involved with dark magic.

"That night, blinded by rage, I cursed every man, woman, and child, from both tribes. I also cursed all of their descendants before taking my own life."

"Which explains why I am cursed," he reasoned aloud.

"Yes, Sunjata. I cursed your ancestors to roam the night, as animals: the Mchanga became lions, and the Misitu became hyenas."

"What will happen?"

"It remains to be seen," she said.

"And Kathleen?"

"I don't know."

"You have summoned all the warriors from both sides. The war will continue."

"Yes, but the end is near."

CHAPTER 16

DR. MEKUFA

"Look! Her tracks stop here," said Lee. Femi stepped on the brakes. Everyone immediately got out. Femi and Hunter knelt down on one knee in the grass while Hanna and Lee stood together, watching them.

The hot sun was bearing down on them. Femi was about to suggest something but stopped when he noticed Hunter pressing his hands on the depressed grass before holding them in front of his face to inhale.

"What are you doing?" asked Hanna, smirking.

Femi stood up and smiled while Lee watched Hunter, amused.

"What? I saw this in a documentary. Trackers do this to find out what type of animal was lying here," defended Hunter. "Right, Femi?"

"Sure," he agreed, trying to hide his amusement.

"And what's your conclusion?" she asked, sceptically.

"One hyena slept over here." He reached over and touched the flattened grass. "Two lay here, and another two lay over there. I'm assuming Kathleen was in the middle."

"Okay, tracker, what happened next?"

The others stepped back and watched as Hunter carefully walked around the area, examining the soil between the tufts of grass.

"The hyenas must have left her, and then someone came and carried her away."

With the mention of someone's footprints, Femi knelt down on one knee beside Hunter to study the tracks he'd found.

"He's right! The footprints are heading toward those rock shelters," he said, pointing to a distant cliff.

"Yeah, looks like he came from the same direction we did," he said.

"But why didn't he carry her back to the site?" asked Lee.

"Maybe she's hurt," suggested Hanna. "Or maybe whoever took her knew we would come looking for her."

"That's if she wasn't abducted," commented Lee.

"Okay, let's not think of the worst," said Hanna.

"Doesn't anyone else here think it's strange that Kathleen was sleeping with a clan of hyenas?" asked Hunter.

"No," the others chortled in agreement, shaking their heads.

"After what we saw last night, I'm willing to believe anything," said Lee.

Femi took off his hat and wiped his forehead. "Why don't we split up? Lee and Hunter, which way do you want to go?" he asked, changing the subject; last night's events were still too fresh in his mind, and all he wanted to do is put all of this behind him.

"We'll go towards the cliff," said Lee.

Hunter, who had pointed in the opposite direction, lowered his arm.

"Okay, we'll head east to see if we can find out where these prints came from," said Femi, straightening his uniform. "I don't get it. There hasn't been anyone in the area besides us. Who could this be?"

"I don't know, but I think we'll find out soon," said Hunter.

"Why do you say that?"

"I got a hunch," he said.

Femi and Hanna began following the prints, which were now harder to see. As they followed the trail, Femi had to backtrack several times to search through the thick turfs for footprints.

After traveling for about a mile, he stopped. "What happened to the tracks?" he asked, stepping back to the last visible prints. "It ends here."

"Look, lion tracks are coming from the same direction," she said. "That's strange! The lion tracks end where the man tracks begin. Do you think—"

"Let's not jump to conclusions. We'd better head back and tell the others we lost the trail," interrupted Femi.

From the look Hanna gave him, he knew she wanted to pursue this discussion, but he felt relieved when she didn't. People shape-shifting into lions just did not happen. He felt solace believing that there was a logical explanation for what he'd seen last night.

* * *

Sunjata looked down at the savannah.

"They have come for Kathleen," said Sunjata.

"Bye, Sun," she said smiling.

Kathleen collapsed in his arms.

"Wake up," he said.

Her head flopped to one side. "Come on, Kathleen, it's almost over. I surely hope you're as stubborn as you have been. Wake, my beauty."

She stirred in his arms. All of a sudden her eyes fluttered open. Sunjata smiled—her eyes were blue. She saw Sunjata and immediately got up and pushed him away.

"Don't touch me," she said, stumbling back.

He caught her.

"Let go of me," she ordered him, pushing his hands away. "What happened to me just now? Why were you holding me?"

"Your friends are here. They have found you," he said.

Kathleen looked down and saw two people in the distance, walking toward them. At first, she couldn't tell who they were, but soon she saw that they were Lee and Hunter. She spun around to say something to Sunjata, but he was gone.

She waved and saw them wave back at her. She descended from the shelter and ran over to them.

"Looks like you're feeling well," said Hunter.

"Where's Sekani?" she asked.

"He had to stay at the site with the others while we went out to search for you," explained Lee. "Let's get you to the jeep first, and then we'll go and find Femi and Hanna."

"Do you have something to eat? I'm starving."

"I have this biscuit," said Hunter as he pulled out a crumbled cookie, still in its wrapper.

Kathleen grabbed it out of his hand, tore the wrapping off, and began devouring it.

They walked over to the jeep and climbed inside to find that Femi had left the keys in the ignition. Hunter started the engine and began driving in the direction Femi and Hanna had gone. They soon spotted their silhouettes in the distance.

"Did you find anything?" Lee asked when they caught up to them.

"No, we lost the trail," he said, looking at Hanna, who gave him a forced smile. He knew what she was thinking, and he was not willing to believe such nonsense.

Femi's cell phone rang.

"Hey, Rick, any luck?"

"That was fast!" Hanna commented.

Femi covered the mouthpiece before explaining, "He knows a lot of people. He's the type of guy who has friends everywhere." He uncovered the mouthpiece "Did you find anything?" he asked.

"Yeah! I met with a couple of Dr. Mekufa's hires. Apparently, he's been paying some guys to cremate the bodies after he's done with his examinations."

"So that no one can prove any different," remarked Femi.

"Exactly, but that's not all. One night, one of the workers forgot his coat, so he went inside and snuck a peek at Dr. Mekufa's journal. From what he read, Dr. Mekufa has been recording that these people died from lion attacks. One of them happened to be his friend's sister; she actually died from malaria."

"But why would he do that?" asked Femi.

"Maybe he has something against lions. If you ask me, all of this is kind of creepy. The guy works in the morgue by candlelight. Oh! I have to go now."

"Thanks, Rick. I owe you one."

"No problem. Anytime, my friend."

"So?" asked Hanna.

"Apparently, he has been writing that all these people died from being attacked by lions, even though that wasn't the case."

"Do you think that Dr. Mekufa is . . . whatever that girl was?" asked Hanna.

"But she was a lioness," reminded Lee.

"Maybe he knows what they are," said Hunter, "and wants to eradicate them."

"That doesn't explain why we were attacked by hyenas," said Lee.

"Do you mind changing the subject?" asked Femi. The thought of the young girl he had killed saddened him and made him feel ill. Femi glanced behind him and noticed Kathleen sleeping in the back, her head resting in Hanna's lap. He shook his head.

"What?" asked Hanna.

"I can't believe how much work one person can be," stated Femi.

"Maybe there is a reason why all of this has been happening to her," said Hanna.

"Well, I think she's a spoiled brat . . . used to getting everything her way. This is her way of getting attention, if you ask me," commented Lee.

"Perhaps, but I think she knows more than she lets on," said Hanna.

Femi's shoulders drooped.

"Are you going to be all right, Femi?" asked Hanna.

"This is the last place I want to go right now," he huffed. He couldn't shake the image of the dead girl.

"I know, Femi. I know," she empathized, reaching out to hold his hand.

They drove along in silence until it became dark. Six bonfires burned brightly in a circle, guiding them.

Kathleen woke up. Okechuku and Sekani ran to her.

"Are you all right?" asked Okechuku.

"Yeah." She smiled, happy to see them.

"What happened to you last night?" asked Okechuku.

"I don't know. I can't remember," she answered, hesitantly. The image of the dead woman flashed in her mind. Her stomach churned before she bolted past the tents to the portable bathroom and threw up.

Kathleen stepped out, walked over to the washbasin, and splashed some water on her face. She felt flushed and disoriented, and as if shards of ice were stabbing at her body.

"Are you okay?" asked Kianga when she noticed how pale she was.

Kathleen looked at her and shook her head before dropping unconscious to the ground. When next she opened her eyes, she saw that she had been tucked inside her sleeping bag with extra blankets placed on top of her.

Dr. Racine placed a thermometer in her mouth and monitored her temperature.

"Impossible!" she exclaimed.

"Does she have a fever?" asked Femi.

Dr. Racine glanced at Femi with a look of concern on her face.

"Quite the contrary, she is as cold as . . ."

". . . a cadaver," interrupted Okechuku.

"Okay, that's enough," said Hanna as she guided the teens out.

"Wait! Sekani!" called out Kathleen in a raspy voice. He noticed that her lips were blue.

"What is it, Kat?" he said, bringing his ear close to her mouth.

"Get everyone to the cave. Tonight," she whispered.

"Tonight?"

"Yeah, before they come," she said.

"Who's coming?" he asked. Sekani looked at her and sighed; Kathleen had fallen asleep.

Sekani walked over to Femi.

"Kathleen told me to get everyone to the cave tonight."

Hanna, Lee, and Hunter stood quietly beside Femi. He glanced at Hanna, who looked equally concerned.

"We'd better warn the professor," Femi decided.

Femi, Hanna, Lee, and Hunter walked over to the professor while Sekani, Okechuku, and Kianga waited by one of the fires.

The professor, who was sitting down and engrossed in a conversation with the coordinator, looked up at the group.

"We have to get everyone to the cave," Femi explained.

"When?" asked the professor, getting up slowly from his chair. The fire cast an orange glow upon their faces.

"Tonight."

"What about the bonfires?" he asked.

"Extra precaution," he said.

The professor took off his hat, ran his hand through his thin hair, and sighed. "Can I get everyone's attention?" he shouted.

The students and staff gathered around him.

"We're going to do something different tonight. I want everyone to gather your backpacks, flashlights, and sleeping bags and head for the cave in Babu Mountain. Okechuku!"

Okechuku stood up and looked at the professor.

"You'll be in charge of making a fire at the entrance to the cave, but not too close—I don't want to smoke you out."

A few teens laughed.

"What about Kathleen?" asked Okechuku.

"I will stay with her," said Dr. Racine.

"I'm staying," announced Sekani.

The professor looked at Femi who in turned nodded to indicate that it was all right with the arrangements.

Okechuku gathered his backpack and a bundle of wood. Adesina and Tanisha approached him.

"Do you need help?" asked Adesina. The girls smiled at him.

"Sure, that would be great," he said excitedly.

Adesina and Tanisha giggled before Adesina grabbed his backpack, allowing Okechuku to carry more wood. Tanisha grabbed a small bundle of wood and glared at Adesina, who got the best end of the deal.

The group, including the remaining of his staff, followed the professor, who had fashioned a torch out of the wood and rags he had saved in his truck. On the mountain ledge, Okechuku, with the help of Adesina and Tanisha, worked on starting the fire while the professor and the students sat around to watch.

By the large tent, Femi, Hanna, Sekani, Lee, and Hunter stared at the bonfires burning brightly.

"What do we do now?" asked Hanna.

"I guess we wait," answered Femi.

"For what?" asked Lee.

"For the hyenas to show up," he said, gripping his rifle firmly.

Femi stepped out into the dark and looked up. A small fire was burning on the mountain. A tall silhouette looked down at them from above; he assumed it was the professor. He then glanced at the savannah, but he couldn't see past the bright lights the fires were emitting.

Femi began kicking dirt and sand on the fires, extinguishing them.

"What are you doing?" asked Lee.

"With this glare, we won't see them coming," he explained.

"*Sisi ona usiku,*" said a low voice from the darkness. Femi turned quickly.

"Senior Elder Gatimu? What are you doing here?" asked Femi, rushing over to greet him and grasping his upper forearms. "*Shikamoo,*" he said. "Hanna, I'd like to meet Senior Elder Gatimu, leader of the Moja tribe. And you brought all the men from your village. *Kwa nini?*" Femi added excitedly.

"Because last night, we saw fire in sky and heard the call of warriors. We come!" explained the elder.

"This is Hanna, Hunter, and Lee," he said, motioning for Hunter and Lee to join them. "And of course, you remember my son, Sekani."

"Ah! Yes, boy strong," he said before smiling.

Sekani walked over to greet him.

"*Ya kupendeza,*" said the elder to Hanna.

Hanna smiled politely.

"He said that you're beautiful," Femi translated.

"Thank you," said Hanna, blushing.

Twenty-five men positioned themselves in the dark. The white markings painted on their faces and bodies gleamed in the moonlight.

With help from Hunter and Lee, Femi and Sekani systematically extinguished the other bonfires, and then they waited.

CHAPTER 17

NJERI'S VERDICT

Sunjata stared at the sunset, waiting for the unbearable pain to rip through his body before subsiding to an aching throb. He closed his eyes and inhaled deeply. How he loved to feel the unbridled strength race through his veins, boundless and free to run wild. With the wind flowing through his thick mane, he lifted his head toward the sky and roared.

*   *   *

"Look!" Femi pointed into the darkness. The men from the Moja tribe silently returned to the elder, obviously unprepared for what was coming.

From the east, red eyes streamed through a sea of swaying grass before merging together out in the open; ten clans of spotted hyenas, led by their matriarch, gathered and faced west. One of the matriarchs stepped forward.

From the west, yellow eyes glimmered as prides of one hundred lions and lionesses marched forward in unison, taking formation in front of the hyenas. One of the lions roared.

The matriarch responded by baring her teeth and snarling.

"What's going on here? What should we do?" asked Femi, pointing to the field with the muzzle of his rifle.

"We do nothing," said the elder. "This is not our battle."

Femi lowered his rifle and looked at the elder.

*   *   *

"What's going on, Professor?" asked Lisha, as they watched the war escalate from Babu Mountain.

"I think we're about to see history in the making," he answered.

*   *   *

"It's time." Kathleen heard Njeri's voice inside her head—or was it her own thoughts? She didn't know anymore.

She slipped out of her bed and walked over to Kianga's shelter box to retrieve Njeri's dagger from her tent. From there, she strode over to her tent and grabbed her leather pouch, containing King Rapula's ashes and the green leather book, before she gracefully walked out onto the field of battle. This was how she remembered the night when Akono died: the moonlight lit the battlefield, and even though the scene seemed as imminent as the night two thousand years ago, it was more subdued, for now, she was in control. They were waiting for her, for she held their future in her hands, and finally she will have her revenge.

The ground-shaking roars and the incessant snarls and cackles died upon her arrival. She walked between the two adversaries and stopped. She turned and faced the lions, thrusting her dagger up into the night; it glimmered before she spun around to face the matriarch of the hyena clans and stared into its eyes.

With the dagger, she drew a large circle around herself in the dirt. She then stabbed it into the hard earth before the matriarch.

She placed the leather book on a patch of grass within the boundaries of the circle, opened the pouch, grabbed a pinch of ash, and began spreading it on the line she had drawn before sprinkling some on the book.

Njeri turned around to face the alpha male lion. She eloquently bowed to the king, placing both hands on her chest before she spoke.

"King Romani, king of the Mashujaa Wa Mchanga tribe, descendant of King Hundo, guardian of the sands, I pledge to you my allegiance."

Upon hearing her words, the hyenas began to pace the ground nervously, cackling and snarling. Njeri looked down and smiled. "How does it feel to be betrayed?" She whispered.

She slowly turned to face the matriarch, raised her right hand, and glared at her. Silence returned. "Queen Nera of the Walinzi Wa Misitu tribe, descendant of King Rapula, slayer of Milele Misitu.

"I, Njeri, daughter of King Rapula, wife of Akono, denounce my allegiance to the Walinzi Wa Misitu tribe." The matriarch bared her teeth. The others of her clan began pacing and snarling while the lions watched in silence.

Njeri knelt down, placed her hand on the dagger's handle and waited. She glared at the matriarch. The hyena growled before lunging at her. Prepared, Njeri plunged her blade into the heart of the hyena. She then knelt before the dying animal and held it by the muzzle. "Thank you, Queen Nera, for without your blood, this next part would have been very difficult." She pulled out the dagger. The matriarch dropped to the ground, panting. She lowered the dagger. The glistening blood ran down the blade, dripping onto the book. The book opened.

Suddenly, the clans attacked. Njeri raised her arms and began shouting an incantation: a wall of blue flames raced along the line she had drawn in the sand. The hyenas stopped and backed away.

Njeri continued, "I, Njeri, sentence you all to a lifetime of imprisonment. You shall never again walk among the living, or in the afterlife, as humans.

You shall crawl, beg, and travel this world with your tail between your legs. The circle of life has ended, and when the darkness falls upon your eyes, you will be forever forgotten. I call upon the forces of my mothers, and all who have lost their lives at the hands of my father, to release the Mashujaa Wa Mchanga from their imprisonment and cast the Walinzi Wa Misitu into an eternity of darkness, until the last scrounging beast walks the earth."

The blue fire transformed into a cold wind, rising into a swirling tornado. Her long black hair twisted and whipped around. As the wind's radius expanded over the savannah, it engulfed both armies, lashing at them violently.

When Njeri lowered her arms, the wind died.

The men and women of the Mashujaa Wa Mchanga tribe got up and looked at one another. No longer were they cursed to roam the night as lions and lionesses. They were warriors again, dressed in their ancient apparel and holding the same weaponry as if they had time travelled back to the night of the war.

King Romani turned to his tribe, raised his staff high into the air and let out a loud shrill. As the tribe shouted in response, Sunjata ran to Njeri, picked her up by the waist, and lifted her up high above his head before letting her down. "You did it."

Njeri smiled.

Suddenly, she heard a whistling sound whizzing by her ear. Something touched her leg before it slid down, dropping at her feet. She turned around and saw that one of the Moja warriors had shot an arrow, killing a hyena in midflight.

As quick as a flash, Sunjata pulled his dagger out of his sheath and spun around on his feet just in time to slice the hyena's throat, saving Kathleen. Within minutes, the Moja tribe had created an impenetrable wall with their spears, protecting them.

The king commanded, "*Tahadhari! Vita nafasi.*"

The Mchanga warriors immediately joined forces with the Moja tribe.

The hyenas paced before them, cackling and snarling, displaying their anger. The warriors took formation and stepped forward, slamming the butts of their spears on the ground.

Defeated, the hyenas ran into the night, leaving Queen Nera, who had finally died from her fatal wound, and two other Misitu warriors laying dead at Njeri's feet, forever cursed in the bodies of hyenas.

Once they were gone, the warriors lowered their weapons.

Njeri approached King Romani. She bowed her head and knelt down on one knee. "Please forgive my people," she said. With open palms, she presented her dagger.

"My people will forever be indebted to you," said the king before taking the dagger. "Thank you."

Sunjata walked over to Njeri.

"How can I ever thank you, Kathleen? Or is it Njeri? I'm so sorry for . . ." His voice trailed off when she placed a finger on his lips. She backed away from him, and smiled. Suddenly, Kathleen's body went rigid before collapsing; Sunjata ran forward and caught her. He scooped her up in his arms and carried her over to Sekani.

"Kathleen is free of Njeri's spirit," said Sunjata.

Sekani took her into his arms and watched Sunjata walk away, surprised by his gesture.

Kathleen looked up in a daze.

"Hey! Here you are! How are you feeling?" asked Sekani.

"Tired."

Sekani placed her upright on the ground, supporting her. Kathleen tried to stand on her own, but her legs were too weak. "Is it all over?" she asked.

"I believe so. You reversed the curse. See, they're all celebrating," he said, but Kathleen was far from feeling exuberant. Instead, she felt confused and exhausted. She saw the king, followed by two of his subjects, approach Femi. One arm wrapped around Sekani's neck, she felt his body become tense.

"Sekani," she said, looking up at him. He glanced down at her. "You should be with your dad."

Sekani nodded at her before walking slowly toward his father, still supporting Kathleen.

"You took the life of my granddaughter," the king said.

Kathleen was saddened to see how much Femi had changed; his gaunt appearance, his red swollen eyes, and the way his body slouched as if the weight of the world was on his shoulders all overwhelmed her with an unbearable guilt. She couldn't help feeling that this was all her fault.

The king placed his hands on his shoulders.

"Do not dwell in the past. You were only protecting this young lady," he acknowledged. Femi glanced at Kathleen, but the look that he gave her was one of contempt. Kathleen looked away, buried her face against Sekani's chest, and began to sob. She welcomed Sekani's strong and warm embrace. She knew how he felt about her, but instead of feeling a sense of relief or joy at being free or compassion and love for Sekani, she felt an unbearable sadness suffocating her and paralyzing her with insecurities and fear. She had witnessed Njeri's pain and lived through the tormented memories of her father, and what she had seen troubled her.

Kathleen looked up and saw Hanna reaching out for Femi's hand while they listened to what the king had to say. Hanna gave her a smile. Kathleen looked away and saw the king's subjects collecting Sade's body.

"What will you do?" asked Femi, looking emotionally drained.

"I imagine there will be a shortage of people at work tomorrow," said the king, smiling.

"Do you mean Dr. Mekufa?" asked Hanna.

"Yes, he is one of many."

"But why did he blame lions for the deaths?" asked Hanna.

"He wanted the Mchanga tribe persecuted. We have been guarding the sands for thousands of years, and we knew the Misitu tribe were trying to find ways to reverse the curse. They planted artefacts cursed with King Rapula's dark magic to take possession of innocent people. But I don't think that anyone had expected someone to find Njeri's grave; little did they know she would turn on them," he explained.

Femi nodded as he listened to the king, but his attention was directed to Kathleen when Hanna squeezed his arms and looked at her. Femi's body became tense, and his jaw clenched.

Kathleen looked at the king. "Excuse me, Your Majesty."

The king looked at her.

"Would you please take Njeri back with you? She needs a proper burial."

The king's expression softened. "Yes, we will take her."

"Can you burn this book and pouch during the burial ceremony?"

She handed him the book and the leather pouch, containing the remnants of the ashes.

"Yes, we will make sure she is well taken care of."

"Thank you."

Senior Elder Gamitu, who was standing beside the king, hollered something in Swahili.

To Kathleen's surprise, she didn't understand a word.

Four men from the Moja tribe carried Njeri's remains toward the king before offering her to him.

"You, girl, strong," said Senior Elder Gatimu to Kathleen. He placed his fist over his heart. "Good inside. We remember."

"Thank you."

"Where you go?" the elder asked the king.

The king looked at his men.

"We shall build a new kingdom."

"We offer, to you and your people, our home in the jungle. You may live with us. It is very quiet," said the elder.

The king pondered the offer before answering. "This is a kind gesture. We would be more than pleased to join with you."

Kathleen turned her attention to Femi, who seemed to be trying really hard to ignore her.

"Mr. Kaita, would you have an axe I could borrow?" she asked.

Femi frowned at her before he strode over to his jeep, grabbed an axe, and handed it to her.

Kathleen marched through the darkness toward the tree.

"What is she doing?" she heard Okechuku ask. The professor and the students had returned from Babu Mountain.

She didn't hear anyone answer his question as she walked away from the torchlights and into the darkness.

Senior Elder Gatimu watched Kathleen disappear. He immediately turned around and spoke to the king, who then ordered his men to create a protective barrier around the bodies of Sade and Njeri. The Moja men grabbed torches and lit them before positioning themselves between the Mchanga warriors. The elder and the king then walked over to the professor and the students.

"Go stand inside," he said, pointing to the Moja tribe and the Mchanga warriors, who were now standing in a circle with their backs to each other.

Unsure of why they needed to follow his instructions, the professor and his students reluctantly entered the circle of warriors.

Sekani returned with two flashlights before handing one to Okechuku; to their dismay, they were escorted inside the protective circle, with the others.

"Can I help?" asked Femi.

"No weapon can help us. Please wait inside."

Femi, Hanna, Hunter, and Lee walked over to the others, apprehensive about the new turn of events.

Suddenly, the elder stopped. He turned around and held out one hand to the people, ordering their silence.

Okechuku crouched down between two warriors' thighs so that he could see what was happening.

"Are you liking the view?" teased Joseph.

Okechuku glanced at him and then at the warriors before he chuckled; the Moja men's apparel consisted of one garment—a leather thong.

The elder carefully walked into the darkness with his staff, the light of the moon illuminating his way.

A loud thud resonated in the night.

"The tree," whispered Okechuku. He spun around to find Kianga, who waved at him from behind the crowd; she seemed frightened. He turned his attention back to where Kathleen had gone.

Another thud echoed in the night, followed by a low moan.

"What was that?" asked Chase.

A light chatter rose from the crowd of onlookers before they all fell silent.

*　*　*

By the light of the moon, Kathleen swung the axe at the tree. With every strike, a low moan emanated from it; the more she cut, the louder it became, until she felt the earth move beneath her feet. She continued chopping at the wood. The blade of her axe finally sliced through the trunk. The tree fell to the ground; the rustling of leaves and the snapping of branches echoed in the night.

Silence fell upon them. Suddenly, Kathleen felt the ground ripple beneath her feet. She gasped and started to back away, forgetting about the grave she had dug. The fall onto her back knocked the wind out of her. A black mist started to exude from the walls. A cold, wet sensation drifted over her body.

She tried to scream, but she felt pressure around her throat as if someone was trying to strangle her. Frozen with fear, she saw inside the mist the face of a man descending upon her, whispering, "It will give me great pleasure to watch you suffocate." The mist reentered the walls, rippling the soil and making the walls collapse onto her. She struggled to free herself from the hold the sand had on her, but it was futile; she was going to die.

She held her breath until she succumbed to the urge to breathe, but the weight on her chest prevented her from inhaling. Her lungs were burning as sand filtered into her nostrils and mouth. She cried, thinking about how she will never see her baby brother or her parents again. She would never know what it would have felt like to fall in love or to be loved. Soon her thoughts transformed to dreams. Then her dreams vanished, and all that remained was emptiness.

"Where's Kathleen?" Sekani squeezed out from behind two Moja warriors, carrying his flashlight as he ran over to the elder.

"*Stop!*" ordered the elder.

They both turned to witness the soil moving before them, as if it were water; wave after wave, the rippling sand started toward them. Sekani froze.

"*Niache!*" the elder shouted, pounding his staff on the ground.

All of a sudden the waves stopped. The sand lifted and moved like a large serpent slithering under the earth.

"It's coming over here!" shouted Okechuku. The group began to panic when the warriors stepped back, forcing everyone closer together.

The earth stopped moving. A black mist diffused out from the ground around them and drifted over their feet, unaffected by the protective shield the Moja tribe had placed around them. A cool, wet sensation wafted over their exposed skin as they tried to move out of its reach.

"Kathleen!" called out Sekani.

He ran over to the grave, jumped in, and placed the flashlight on the ground.

"Kathleen," Sekani glided his hands over the ground, but all he could find was sand. "Help!" he shouted as he began digging. He sank to his knees and ran his hands through his hair, feeling completely overwhelmed with despair. *"Help!"*

Okechuku jumped in.

"I can't find her! I can't find her!" he screamed.

"We'll find her! We'll find her!" reassured Okechuku.

On their knees, Sekani and Okechuku dug with their hands as fast as they could. The light from the torches and flashlights from the others who came to help lit the grave. The professor jumped in and began digging.

"I can't find her," said Sekani. Femi jumped in and grabbed his son's shoulder.

"You did your best," he said.

"No, I didn't. This cannot end this way! We have to find her," he said, tearing away from his grip.

They continued digging with their hands.

"I found her!" Okechuku shouted. He had found her T-shirt.

Sekani and the professor joined him and began concentrating in one section. Finally, they had unburied her. Okechuku gasped; he thought he had seen shadows of hands holding Kathleen's wrist before disappearing into the ground.

"She's not breathing!" shouted Sekani.

They pulled her out and laid her on the ground outside the hole.

"Kathleen!" Sekani shouted.

Femi dropped to his knees beside him.

"Dr. Racine!" shouted the professor. "Give her some room," he ordered.

Dr. Racine, who had been watching, knelt down beside her, turned her onto her side, and began sweeping her mouth with her finger to remove the sand. She then began giving her artificial respiration.

Okechuku looked at Kianga, who looked as worried as he felt. She walked over to Sekani and placed a hand on his shoulder.

After the doctor's fifth attempt to resuscitate her, Kathleen coughed, gasping heavily for air. Suddenly, her hair slowly changed from black to blonde, as if black ink was bleeding out from each strand into the ground, until nothing remained except for her natural colour.

Sekani and Okechuku hugged her.

After taking several deep breaths, she whispered, "I heard him."

"Who?" asked Sekani.

"King Rapula."

Kathleen tried to stand, but her legs were too weak. With Sekani and Okechuku's help, she walked over to where Njeri's body had been resting.

Kathleen entered the area where the Moja warriors had been moments ago. The elder, the king, Sekani and Sunjata followed her. Kathleen lifted the sheets that had been covering Njeri and fell to her knees.

Everyone watched her.

A pair of hands rested on her shoulders; it was Senior Elder Gatimu. Kathleen stood up to look at him, her legs trembling.

"You have done all that you could have," he said.

"What happened?" asked Okechuku.

"She's gone," she explained.

The king walked over to Kathleen. "I am sorry to say her dagger, book, and pouch are gone as well."

Sekani looked at Sunjata, who was approaching Kathleen to console her.

Sekani placed an arm around her, challenging him. Sunjata raised his hands submissively.

"He has Njeri. I failed her," she said before she buried her face into Sekani's chest and cried.

Later, they watched the Moja and Mchanga tribes as they carried Sade's body, headed north past the mountains while chanting a low mourning rhythm, their torches burning brightly.

After several minutes, Okechuku startled Kathleen by hugging her tightly.

Femi and Hanna spun around to look at them, shocked.

"Thank you, Kat! Without you, this whole experience would have been painfully boring," he said.

Everyone began to laugh.

"What do you mean, boring?" asked the professor, who had overheard Okechuku.

"Ah, don't worry, Professor! I'm sure it would have been a great lesson without all the distractions. Maybe next year . . ." said Amber.

"Next year? Do you think after what you guys put me through that I'm going to teach another class? I'm retiring and going back home," he said with certainty.

The class cheered.

The professor couldn't help but laugh as several of his students gave him heart-warming hugs.

Suddenly, a jeep approached them.

"What now?" Femi groaned.

The vehicle stopped, and a white woman climbed out of her jeep. Her tousled hair suggested that she had experienced an interesting night of her own. She limped over to the professor.

"Dr. Blackwell!" shouted the professor.

"I'm sorry, Adrian. You wouldn't believe the night I've been having. First, I had a flat tire, and then a pack of hyenas wouldn't let me out of my vehicle. When they lost interest, I think I sprained my ankle while trying to get help . . ." her voice trailed off when she noticed a stream of light disappear behind some trees in the distance.

"I've missed everything, haven't I?" she asked.

"Yep, but think of it this way. Your hypothesis about the Misitu artefacts and their relation to the recent killing was bang-on," explained the professor.

"I was . . . how?"

"I'll explain later," said the professor.

"Okay," she agreed, trying to untangle her messy hair.

CHAPTER 18

GOOD-BYES

Kathleen sat on a ledge on Babu Mountain, watching the other teens below converse with each other while slowly packing their belongings in preparation to leave.

Professor Holdsworth spent most of his time recounting all the events leading to last night, comparing theories with Dr. Blackwell, and trying to make sense of what had happened.

The kitchen crew had returned to disassemble the tents for the dining area and kitchen, collected their equipment and supplies, and loaded it into a large white cube van, setting aside a small supply of rations for the staff and students who would be staying for one more night. Without so much as a glance, they were gone.

Chase, Adesina, Amber, Sadia, Tanisha, Lisha, and her brother Joseph kept to themselves, laughing and jostling around with each other. The girls who had given up on Sekani were spending a lot more time with Okechuku, who seemed to be enjoying the attention. Kathleen wished that she could be more like him; it didn't matter what horror or challenges he'd encountered, he always found a way to shrug it off and make light of the situation.

She saw Sekani pacing along the site. He was withdrawn and didn't say much to anyone. Kathleen felt disheartened, as she believed she was to blame for all that had happened, and she felt responsible for changing their lives. She hoped that Sekani would return to his dream of running in the Olympics—maybe in time he would.

Kathleen watched the others. She felt alienated from everyone, an outcast like Njeri. People avoided her or kept their distance. Yet, she welcomed the tranquility. She too, felt withdrawn, not wanting to do anything or speak to anyone.

Even though she was exhausted, she didn't want to sleep. After being buried alive, she feared the darkness, as if the walls would close in on her whenever she closed her eyes.

The night before, Dr. Racine had given her something to help her sleep while remaining by her side with Sekani. Whenever she woke up screaming, Sekani held her hand while Dr. Racine stroked her forehead, whispering softly to her as if she was a child.

A tear trickled down her cheek. She watched Okechuku pack the poles of his tent into his bag; she was going to miss him. But there was something more. It felt as if traces of Njeri's emotions and memories had made an impression, branding her soul and shadowing her thoughts. A lingering sadness had draped over her. No matter how much she tried to be optimistic, her thoughts spiralled downwards—maybe with time she would recover.

She watched Adesina walk over to Okechuku; she definitely liked him. They looked up at Kathleen before he sauntered away.

After several minutes, she heard his footsteps approaching.

"Why didn't you stay with her?" she asked.

"Why are you sitting up here, all alone?"

"Isn't that what everyone wants?" she replied.

"No," he said.

Kathleen looked at him; her eyes were red and glassy.

"Kat, what's wrong?" asked Okechuku.

"So much has happened. I'm just trying to make sense of it all," she explained.

"When is your dad picking you up?" asked Okechuku.

"Tomorrow," replied Kathleen. Her voice quivered.

"What's wrong?" he pleaded with her.

"I've never felt like I belonged until I came here, and because of you, Oke, I feel like the luckiest girl in the world to have made a friend like you," she confessed.

"I feel the same way, Kat. You're my best friend," he said, grabbing her by the shoulders and giving her a hug. He grabbed her chin and gently made her look at him, "Don't you think that just because we are separated by distance that I won't keep in touch. I have your e-mail address, and you can count on receiving several e-mails a day, especially during history class," he finished with a smile.

Kathleen laughed. She wiped the tears away with the back of her hand. "I thought that would be your favourite subject," she said, sniffling.

"After what happened here, I think I got enough of a history lesson to last a lifetime."

Another tear trickled down her cheek.

Okechuku gave her another bear hug.

"Why don't you come and visit next summer? Maybe my dad will let us ride with him on the steamboat," he suggested.

"That would be great," she agreed before wiping her eyes again. "My dad travels in the US often. I'm sure I can convince him to take me along," she added.

"What's going to happen between you and Sekani?" he asked.

"I don't know," she said, glancing at Sekani, who was speaking to his dad.

In the distance, a school bus approached. "I guess I'd better get down," he said before standing up.

"Do you think I'll ever forget?"

"If you mean forgetting about what happened to you, maybe in time you will. C'mon, let's head back down," he said. She didn't respond. "C'mon, Kat." He took her hand. "It will get better," he said, while guiding her by the hand.

At the campsite, Okechuku chuckled, "Oh! No! Not that old broken-down piece of junk!" A loud screech pierced their ears when the bus came to a stop. The driver turned the engine off.

"I guess this is it!" he announced.

Kathleen hugged him hard. Fresh tears streamed down her face. She stepped back and gave him a smile.

Sekani sauntered forward, gave her a hug, and handed her a tissue before giving Okechuku a one-armed hug, each patting the other on the back.

"You take care of yourself!" said Sekani.

"Yeah! You too! We'll see you around," he said before grabbing his backpack, sleeping bag, and tent. He entered the bus and found a seat at the back. He watched them from his window.

Chase, Adesina, Lisha, Amber, Sadia, Tanisha, and Joseph slowly streamed onto the bus, finding their seats as they chattered loudly, laughing and cajoling.

Adesina sat beside Okechuku. "Are you excited to go home?" she asked.

"Yeah, I am," he said before glancing at Kathleen, who was standing beside Sekani.

"Hey, Buttercup!" said Kianga. "Nice to see you blonde again."

"Thanks," said Kathleen.

Sekani sauntered away.

"I want you to have this." Kianga handed her a delicate carving of a flower, similar to the one she had found resting on her pillow.

Kathleen looked at her, surprised. "Did you make this?"

"Yeah." She glanced away, looking uncomfortable.

"It's beautiful."

"Yeah, yeah. If I were you, I wouldn't go digging anymore," she said before turning around and walking toward the bus.

Suddenly, a thought occurred to her. "Kianga?"

Kianga stopped to look at Kathleen.

"Were you the one who gave me that flower?" she asked.

Kianga rolled her eyes and walked back to her. She then leaned over so that no one could overhear. "I know you won't let this go, so . . . yeah, I did. You needed some cheering up. Personally, I'd hoped you thought it came from Sekani. He has a thing for you, you know," she said before she walked over to the bus.

"Thanks," Kathleen called out to her.

"Don't mention it, Buttercup! See ya around!" Without looking back, she waved at Kathleen before entering the bus; her thin, tightly rolled blanket tucked under her arm held the only possessions she owned: two T-shirts and a jack knife.

Thinking back, Kathleen suddenly realized how difficult life had been for Kianga. She had lost her parents and had been living in one foster home after another. But most of the time, she found herself running away and living in the streets.

Her brothers survived by stealing and selling drugs. They often stopped by, collecting the money she had made from odd jobs or from her woodcarvings she had sold.

Kathleen felt ashamed, for every time it rained, Kianga had disappeared, but it was only now that Sekani had told her that Kianga had gone to lay down in her shelter box so that she could keep her blanket dry. She looked back at Sekani, who had stepped back to give her some privacy when she was speaking to Kianga, and walked over to him.

"Sekani, what's going to happen to Kianga?"

"Michelle has offered to take her into her home in Nairobi for the time being while the court determines what to do with her."

Michelle, Sade, and Dr. Racine were the next to board. Dr. Racine stopped, smiled, and waved at Kathleen before continuing.

Kathleen glanced at Okechuku; another wave of sadness washed over her.

He got up, stuck his head out of his window, and hollered, "Check your e-mail when you get home. We'll chat soon. Have a good trip!" he yelled. The bus drove away.

Professor Holdsworth and Dr. Blackwell proceeded to make lunch. Femi and Hanna walked away holding hands while Hunter and Lee were sitting down playing a game of cards. Sekani stood beside Kathleen as she watched the bus drive off.

"I can't believe it! Has it already been a month?" asked Kathleen. "So much has happened."

"Kat, it has only been two weeks. Because of everything that has happened, the professor decided to cancel the program," explained Sekani.

"I'm sorry!"

"Don't worry about it! Everyone seemed quite excited about leaving," he said.

Kathleen signed, feeling very disappointed.

"Where are you going?" asked Sekani.

"I just remembered something."

She walked over to her backpack and withdrew Apana's diary before heading toward Dr. Blackwell, whose blonde hair had been neatly brushed and was gathered loosely in a barrette; a few strands cascaded along her narrow face as she was preparing sandwiches.

"Excuse me, Dr. Blackwell."

"Hello, Kathleen. Are you hungry?"

"No, not really," she answered.

"Oh! She will have something," said Sekani.

Kathleen glared at him.

"What? Someone has to take care of you," he explained.

"Whatever," she said dismissively.

"I have something you may want," she said, handing over the diary.

"What's this?" asked the doctor.

"It's Apana's diary . . . Njeri's untold story."

Professor Blackwell's eyes widened with curiosity and excitement.

"How did you get this?"

"A woman in Kanzikuta Village gave it to me."

Dr. Blackwell leafed through it quickly. "Thank you very much, Kathleen. I will keep it safe, and I will make sure that her true story is known," she said.

"Thank you. She would have wanted that."

"Kathleen, did you want to talk about what happened?"

"If you don't mind, Dr. Blackwell, I'd rather not."

"All right. I'm here if you change your mind," she said before she walked over to a folding chair with a plate of food, sat down, and began reading.

Kathleen sauntered over to where the twisted tree once stood; a charred hole was all that remained. Black soot and ash discoloured the soil where the tree had fallen—the tree had turned to ash overnight.

She sat alone, her knees drawn up to her chest. Sekani brought her a sandwich and waited for a moment, and when she didn't reach over to take it, he placed it beside her on the ground before sitting down next to her.

She watched the red, blazing sun as it touched the horizon. She admired its beauty: Kathleen couldn't remember the last time she had stopped to watch the sunset in Canada, but she knew the next time she did, her thoughts would be of Kenya.

"It's beautiful, isn't it?"

"Yeah! Mesmerizing," agreed Sekani.

She sighed at the thought of going home. She missed her family, especially her younger brother, and she missed sleeping in her own bed. Soon she would be going back to school, back to her superficial, so-called friends, back to the same boring routine, but at least she would be safe at home, surrounded by love ones and comforted by all the things she used to take for granted.

Even though she had been well treated at the archaeological site, she had witnessed through the eyes of Njeri how cruel and unfair life could be.

"Do you want to join us by the fire?" asked Sekani, snapping her out of her daydream.

"Sure." She got up and kicked her plate of food by accident. "Oops." She picked it up and headed over to the warm fire. She dumped her sandwich into the fire and placed her plate under her chair.

"You know, Hunter, nobody is ever going to believe what happened here," said Lee.

"I know."

"What do we do now?" asked Lee.

"We go back to studying lions."

Who would believe me if I told anyone at home? she thought as she overheard Lee and Hunter talking.

She watched Hanna sitting beside Femi, her head resting on his shoulder while they held hands.

"I never told Vanessa how much she meant to us. She practically raised Sekani," whispered Femi. Hanna listened.

The roar of a lion in the distance pierced the darkness, shattering Kathleen's sense of security; her heart began to race. Everyone looked at her when she jumped.

Sekani got a blanket and sat on it before grabbing her hand, guiding her to sit in front of him. She leaned back against him. He wrapped his arms around her, making her feel safe and snug. He held her tightly and kissed the back of her head.

Though afraid to fall asleep, she felt comforted by Sekani strong arms holding her.

She glanced across the fire and saw Hanna smiling at them and Femi scowling at her before she stared once again at the fire.

"Will I ever see you again?" asked Sekani.

"I don't think so," she answered.

After a long moment of silence, Kathleen started to speak. "Sekani?"

"What?"

"When I was under the influence of Njeri, I had the opportunity to see her memories. I saw what happened to her, but not only that, I felt her pain, her hatred, her anguish, and her lust for revenge."

Everyone was sleeping except Hunter, who had been listening quietly to what she said, glancing at her for a moment with an empathetic expression on his face before returning his gaze to the orange blaze.

"Sekani, I'm scared."

"Why?"

"For one thing, King Rapula is free . . . and I don't think we've heard the last of him."

"What do you think will happen to Njeri?"

"I don't know. I think she is still very angry and tormented."

"You will be going home and putting this all behind you."

"I hope."

"I want to see you again, Kat."

"I know."

They sat in silence, enjoying each other's company.

The next morning, she was awoken by the sound of a vehicle approaching. She looked up to see that her father had arrived.

"Sekani," she whispered. They had fallen asleep sitting together, his arms wrapped around her shoulders; to her surprise, she had slept peacefully.

Sekani woke with a start.

"It's okay. My dad is here."

Sekani got up, slapped the dust off his jeans and grabbed Kathleen's backpack before walking over to meet her father.

"Dad!" she shouted as she ran to him, giving him a big hug.

"I missed you too, honey!" He greeted her, surprised by all the sudden affection.

"This is Sekani," she said.

They shook hands. Professor Holdsworth walked over to greet Mr. Gallant while Femi and the others were having breakfast.

"Professor."

"Mr. Gallant."

"Sorry to hear that the program was cancelled."

"You will receive a partial refund in the mail," explained the professor.

"Did you find anything?" asked her father.

The professor looked at Kathleen, took off his hat, and scratched his face. Kathleen shook her head slightly. *Please don't tell*, she pleaded silently.

"I'm afraid . . ."

Kathleen held her breath.

"I'm afraid we didn't find many artefacts."

Kathleen silently sighed in relief. The professor gave her a smile.

"That's too bad. Maybe better luck next time."

"She did find this flint dagger." He pulled out the dagger from his pocket and handed it to her. "You can keep it. I won't be needing it anymore."

"Thank you, Professor."

"All right, then . . . are you ready to go?" he asked.

"Sure am!" answered Kathleen excitedly.

"Take care of yourself. Maybe I will see you in London," said the professor before walking away.

"Yeah! Sure!"

She turned to look at Sekani when her heart started to ache; most of the time they had spent together she had been under Njeri's spell. Under different circumstances, she might have fallen for him. She was grateful that he had been part of her life, for he had saved her life several times, and he was one of the few who'd never given up on her.

She walked over to him and kissed him gently on the lips. "Thank you, Sekani. I will never forget what you did for me. Maybe we will see each other again. Here's my phone number and e-mail address." She slipped a piece of paper into his hand before getting into the car.

Her dad patiently waited for her, seeming uncomfortable with seeing his daughter kissing a boy.

Sekani handed her her backpack.

"I look forward to seeing you again," he replied.

Kathleen smiled at him. He stepped back and watched as the car drove off; he knew he'd never forget her, and he was already looking forward to the day they would meet again.

Suddenly, he felt a hand on his shoulder.

"All ready for the drive, sport?" asked Femi.

"Yeah!" He grabbed his things, opened the hatch to his father's jeep, and loaded them inside before shutting it. He sat in the backseat beside Lee and Hunter. Hanna then climbed into the front seat. They waved at the professor and Dr. Blackwell, who were also getting ready to leave. The only proof that there had been an archaeological camp was the sign and the upturned earth. Hidden amongst the golden grass, several feet away from the site, lay the bodies of Queen Nera and two other hyenas—descendants of the Misitu tribe—buried in shallow graves.

They drove away in silence; Femi mourned the loss of a good friend and Sekani of a mother figure. Vanessa's funeral was being held at the Nasiche Wildlife Sanctuary that afternoon. They planned to attend and pay their respects.

Femi turned the radio on.

". . . are puzzled as to why ten percent of the workforce didn't show up for work on Thursday. Dr. Mekufa, a renowned coroner from Nairobi, is one of the people who've gone missing. While authorities are concerned about the disappearances, no foul play is suspected at this time."

Femi switched off the radio.

"Like I always say," reminded Femi with a smirk, "don't believe everything you hear."

They all laughed.

The End